Prizm Books

Aisling: Book I Guardian by Carole Cummings
Aisling: Book II Dream by Carole Cummings
Aisling: Book III Beloved Son by Carole Cummings
Changing Jamie by Dakota Chase
City/Country by Nicky Gray
Comfort Me by Louis Flint Ceci
Desmond and Garrick Book I by Hayden Thorne
Desmond and Garrick Book II by Hayden Thorne
Devilwood Lane by Lucia Moreno Velo
Don't Ask by Laura Hughes
Eagle's Peak by Elizabeth Fontaine
The End by Nora Olsen
Foxhart by A.R. Jarvis
Heart Sense by KL Richardsson
Heart Song by KL Richardsson
I Kiss Girls by Gina Harris
Ink ~ Blood ~ Fire by K. Baldwin & Lyra Ricci
Josef Jaeger by Jere' M. Fishback
Just for Kicks by Racheal Renwick
The Next Competitor by K. P. Kincaid
Repeating History: The Eye of Ra by Dakota Chase
The Second Mango by Shira Glassman
A Strange Place in Time series by Alyx J. Shaw
The Strings of the Violin by Alisse Lee Goldenberg
The Suicide Year by Lena Prodan
Tartaros by Voss Foster
The Tenth Man by Tamara Sheehan
Tyler Buckspan by Jere' M. Fishback
Under the Willow by Kari Jo Spear
Vampirism and You! by Missouri Dalton
The Water Seekers by Michelle Rode
The World's a Stage by Gail Sterling

Eagle Peak

Elizabeth Fontaine

Eagle Peak

Eagle Peak
PRIZM
An imprint of Torquere Press, Inc.

1380 Rio Rancho Blvd #1319, Rio Rancho, NM 87124.
Copyright 2014 © by Elizabeth Fontaine
Cover illustration by BSClay
Published with permission
ISBN: 978-1-61040-673-4
www.prizmbooks.com
www.torquerepress.com

First Prizm Printing: March 2014
Printed in the USA

www.prizmbooks.com

Eagle Peak

Elizabeth Fontaine

Eagle Peak

This book is dedicated to my father, who wrote fearlessly throughout his life and passed on the necessity to me, and to Michael, Pearl, Lily and Lucas, who support me with the love and humor necessary for this wife and mom to take the time to write and not be in a constant state of guilt.

Thank you to Angry Catfish Bicycle Shop and Coffee Bar, for letting me write an entire novel on their premises while only buying one small latte at a time—granted, it has been a LOT of lattes. Another thank you to my mom, Larisa, Sophie, Cecilia, Rachel, Katy, Alex, Maiya and Michael (again) for reading, hearing and providing feedback on all manner of drafts. And a final thank you to all my friends and colleagues for all the encouraging words and inspiration.

Eagle Peak

Chapter 1: Bars

Mom is as perky as Sarah's tits, and I don't mean that in some weird Freudian way. She is marching around like a manic ant, and Sarah's tits kind of stand at attention because they are so small. I'm not complaining. They are nice and she is the only girl who's ever let me feel them, so what do I really know?

"Doesn't it just feel great to scale down now and then?" Mom says, handing me a box of one of our most treasured family heirlooms—the Kung Fu movie collection. "I probably brought four car loads of stuff to Goodwill last week," Mom says. "We are back down to exactly what we need, aren't we, See-see?"

I sigh at her use of my nickname, a perversion of my real name Sean, spelled normally but pronounced See-an. I've gotten used to explaining this, and have come to prefer it to her nickname. But she slings her arm around my waist and pulls me into her, her head resting on my shoulder. "How'd you get so tall?"

"It's all relative, Mom. You are just really really short. I'm pretty average."

She swings me around and holds onto my hands in one of those awkward embraces she loves to embarrass me with and says, "There's nothing average about you."

Like that is supposed to be some kind of a comfort.

"Don't you forget that," she says more seriously this time, pulling her hand up to my face to run it under my right eye. It's her habit, to fix my eyeliner.

I walk back to the house to grab more boxes but end up in the living room. It looks so empty. Not that I'll miss it. Like every other place my parents and I have lived, this is a rental, so that means we never get too attached. But we have always stayed rooted in Minneapolis, so moving to a small town in Central Minnesota, a "rural community," to use Dad's words, just really sucks. I am beyond the shock that the only jobs in the universe that my parents could find are in a town called Eagle Peak. Mom's claim that these jobs are the "universe directing us on a new adventure" is not soothing. The bottom line is they are taking me away from my friends and an almost girlfriend two weeks into the school year.

"Bye," I text into my prehistoric phone. You know, the kind that you have to hit the "2" button two times for a "b," and don't even get me started on thumb cramping due to having to push too hard. One day perhaps I'll have an intellectually superior phone that punctuates my sentences, but that's not in the cards yet. Even if my parents' new jobs work out, who would I text? I'm losing all my friends anyway. I don't expect a reply even though it went out to six people, one of whom is my best friend, Trenton. I look at my phone. Nothing.

As if on cue, I hear a car stop in our driveway and look out to see my loud friends piling out the window. Trenton saw this in a movie once and thought it looked cool, so he is forever trying to figure out the suavest way to exit a car via window. He has almost managed it, head first and then awkward hand flip, but Ben, trying to go like Trenton, ends up landing mostly on his neck while the others practically step on him on their way out. They look like idiots, and I laugh. Then I have tears in my eyes like a big baby.

Trenton finds me standing in the empty living room

and then he does it—puts me in my second awkward embrace of the day and starts crying. Crying, like it's him moving and not me. But we've been friends since junior high, so maybe this sucks for him too. I stand there and comfort my best friend in a tight hug the same way I held him when he went through his break-up with his latest boyfriend—there are too many to count. And then I find myself clinging to him like my life relies on it, and then I'm crying too, quiet, not loud and sobbing like Trenton does. He steps back and looks me in the eyes and says, "Well, my work here's done."

"You asshole," I say wiping under my eyes.

"Just text us, take pictures of the cute farm boys, call if you are really hard up, and when you come back every weekend...party!" Jazz hands. Only Trent can pull that off and look good.

"They'll all be Abercrombie & Fitch girls at best," I say.

"Then perhaps you should just fess up and get gay—I bet there are some real hard body farmer boys!" he squeals, clapping his hands. God, I'll miss that. On girls it is annoying, but on Trenton, it's endearing.

His "get gay" nagging is both comforting and grating. He knows we can't choose who we're hot for as well as anyone, but it doesn't stop him from harassing me. We're best friends though, so I put up with him. I can't stop myself from tearing up again when I think about that, about all the things we've been through together.

He gives me the famous Trenton head cock and says, "Ah, See. It'll be okay. We'll still love you in overalls."

I snort at that. He can always make me laugh.

"Now we're going to bring in the big guns," and then he turns to the door and screams, "Sarah!"

"No," I groan and quickly wipe more tears away.

Sarah walks in looking almost shy, like she has a shy

bone in her gorgeous body. Trenton walks out and gives Sarah a meaningful look, which she ignores as she walks right up to me and kisses me hard, like really hard and not at all girly, and it's a turn-on.

By the time I walk out of the damned house with Sarah, I have puffy eyes and a monster boner, which is not the image I want to be memorialized with. My friends are lined along the driveway acting out some morbid kind of funeral scene. Trenton is wheezing into a hanky, and Ben and Leroy are moaning and crying out on the grass, rolling pathetically back and forth, and granted, it's kind of funny. So I continue my death march to the car as Sarah takes her place as one of the mourners, but she just stands there.

As we pull onto Hiawatha Avenue, I have no other words other than my heart is completely breaking. I want to cry, but I don't. Mom keeps looking back. I can tell she feels bad, and I am not going to let her off, so I just sit and glare out the window. I blink as we drive past Lake Street where I spend Mondays shopping at Savers for dollar tag days, the Dollar Tree where we get our pink hair dye for Valentine's Day, Cedar neighborhood where I take acting classes at Mixed Blood, well, used to. I continue to blink until we drive under the Lowry tunnel, past North Minneapolis, beyond the subdivisions with their McMansions that my friends and I always scoff at.

Pretty soon I am flooded with texts.

Trenton: ms u lrdy.

He thinks he's clever with his texting shorthand. "Merging two great literary techniques," he likes to say.

Ben: Have fun!

Yeah, as if.

Leroy: Come home.

I don't even really know Leroy all that well, but it's sweet anyway.

Sarah: Asshole.

Typical. Then another.

Sarah: I'll wait for you.

Damn. More tears. I put the phone down and lean my forehead against the window watching the ditch go by like I used to do as a kid.   When the billboards begin to thin out, I ask the one question that I know will annoy my parents. "Are we there yet?"

Dad squints his eyes at me through the rearview mirror. I take a close up of myself looking, I think, like I'm dying, which I am. My screen is too small to really see the picture, but I send it to everyone anyway.

I put in my ear buds to drown out the drone of the road with Trenton's old MP3 player. It's his music, so I'm surprised when I see my name as a playlist. I hit shuffle and Jimmy Buffet, something he never ever listens to, comes on singing about playing all day. I don't get it at all and it's painful, so I hit forward. Then "I Love Rock & Roll" comes on and I get it. Classic rock. It's kinda funny, and it's also a little touching that Trent put time into making me a classic rock playlist.

There is not much to look at around here. It's almost sterile. Just fields, some woods, billboards, and an occasional exit ramp that leads to some pathetic dive town or another. My eyes close in utter boredom.

I wake up later because Dad is exiting. We enter a place called Sauk Center. "Home of Sinclair Lewis" the sign proudly boasts. Interesting. Didn't he write something about Main Street? I should look him up. Then I wonder out loud, "Do they even have a library in this town?"

"In fact, they do," Mom says and turns to Dad like there's some kind of a joke.

"What? What's the joke, guys?"

They just bust out laughing. God!

"You'll see. It's kind of a surprise."

"Christ!" I mumble. This is hell.

After forty-five minutes, I am beyond desperate riding through town after town that begins and ends with farm fields, watching the bars on my phone disappear, sometimes vanishing altogether. Every town we drive through is made up of four to six blocks that contain about ten houses, a grocery store as small as the Corner Mart down our old block, two or three churches, a gas station, a truck stop or café, and a couple of liquor stores. There is never anything closely resembling a coffee house or even a movie theater. It's just trashy. I don't like to judge things, but there is no personality in the buildings and there is absolutely nothing pleasing to look at. The two people I actually see out of their car walking on a street are old and they look like they are farmers, whatever that looks like. I get more and more pissy with every town we pass. They are towns with old lady's names like Bertha, Clarissa, Estherville. Really? Was the ville really necessary? Some have incredibly boring names, like Long Prairie or Prairieville as if the prairie wasn't obvious enough.

"We're almost there," Mom says. She almost sounds nervous, but I figure she should be. The pit in my stomach hurts, and I blame her and Dad. How could they do this to me?

The first thing off the highway that signifies another populace of people is this overgrown field of junked cars, dating from the dawn of the wheel to present. Beyond the rusted cars is a huge mountain of gravel.

"Let me guess," I grunt. "Eagle Peak?"

They don't get my joke though and just nod at a sign: "Eagle Peak Population 596." Shit, I had more kids in my class at South than this entire town.

"And now we are coming up to the gas station, 'Shirley's'. Sean, I'll bet you'll never guess the owner's name!" I can tell this is a joke; she's terrible at punch lines because she always gives it away.

"Hmm, Mom. Let me see. Could it be Shirley?"

"I don't know actually," she says, like I am curious. "I haven't asked yet, but the café on Main Street is called Mike's, and I do know for a fact that Mike Bentz is the owner."

"Fascinating," I say, making sure to say it right, so they know I don't want to talk.

We drive past Eagle Peak Truck Stop and a park, at least that is what I assume it is—three swings attached to a tall bar, a tall metal slide, and a picnic table. There are three churches, and a bunch of houses. We get to a street called "Main Street" down which I see a lot more businesses. My phone has no fucking bars.

And then we turn the other way and begin to climb a really long tall hill. It surprises me. It has been so flat up to this point. Hardly a "peak," but impressive nonetheless.

"And here comes the school, where we will be spending our days!" Dad says chuckling.

"Oh honey," Mom says, "poor Sean has enough to worry about without you bringing up our, well, proximity?" And then she turns to me. "But Sean, you are going to love this school as much as your father and I love it. I know you will. It is stunning."

"An art deco masterpiece!" pipes in my father.

At that, the trees open up to a massive cement structure, three stories tall and almost a block wide. It is a monstrosity. I laugh a little because the building looks more like a high security prison than a 7-12 school.

"The outside is infinitely less interesting than the inside. Wait till you see it. You will love the auditorium!" She says.

We turn again, and I can see a wooden section of the school stretching out beyond the cement. The sign on the windows says, "Proud of our FFA State Winners!!!"

"What is FFA?" I ask.

"Future Farmers of America," Mom says, clearly impressing herself.

"Ugh," I say, wincing at the idea of it. Future farmers are the pride and joy of this school. I mean, not like I have anything against farmers. I like to eat as much as anyone else, but I know that I don't want to be one of them, and I can't imagine what some farmer kid and I would talk about.

"And there, you see that other addition?" Dad asks.

"Yes?" I say nervously.

"That is the Ag. Department and the shop studio."

"Shop. Studio? As in a studio where they cut and hammer things?" Please, let the madness stop!

"They build things," Dad says, sounding defensive. Of course this is something he would appreciate. His idea of a good time is rewiring the electricity or building a bookcase or something, and I'm sure he is excited about the prospect of a huge, and I mean huge, space for working in. But a guy can only take so much.

"Mmhmm," I say beginning to need to tune out again. I look down at my phone and crank my music, one bar. Can you even send a text with one bar? I try. "Help," I send to Trenton. I'd add an exclamation point if it were an option!

We turn into the parking lot of the school, drive all the way around the huge cement structure and make our way back down the big hill. Going down the long hill I can see about five blocks ahead and notice a lot of trees that are starting to turn that fall yellow color, big old houses with porches, and wide streets with sidewalks.

"Grain Elevators," my Dad says pointing at the two round towers a few blocks away. I have no idea what a grain elevator does and I don't want to learn so I look out the window. A couple people are out in their yard. One kid is biking. And then we turn again, and again, and then I can tell we are "downtown."

Two blocks later we pull over in front of the library, which is clearly closed. I shut off my music, notice my phone is "searching," get out of the car, and look around. The block is dense with old brick buildings of varying heights and colors, the awnings stretching out in front announcing the names—Eagle Peak Liquor, Eagle Peak Library, Eagle Peak Senior Citizens Center, Eagle Peak Bank. Nope, no way I could forget I am in Eagle Peak. I turn around and see Mike's café, Eagle Peak Farm Supply, Eagle Peak Lions Club, and then just "Grocery." Who are these people?

And then I have a new thought. "Wait, what's up with all these businesses? There are like less than 600 people here."

Mom and Dad share another look.

"I guess it gets to be pretty isolated, so they have to have all their bases covered," Dad says, clearly making this shit up as he goes.

"Isolated," I say, "Yeah, right." And then like that my curiosity is gone and I'm left with only my annoyance.

I wish Mom and Dad would just show me our new house, so I could hole up and stare at a blank wall and listen to my music. Please let us live on a hill where I can get some kind of signal. I am sure this is the beginning of depression. How could I not get depressed given my situation? Then I think about Trenton and the days he spends in bed after a break-up and realize I could never be that desperate. I look again at the library in front of me and say, "Okay, so they have a library. What's the big joke?"

"No joke, Sean," answers Mom, trying to hide the excitement in her voice. "This is our new home."

"Yes, Mother, I get that. We live in Eagle Peak now. God, how could I forget!" I wave my hands at all the storefronts to make my point.

"No, Sean, this," and she points at the library, "is our home."

"Um, Mom, I think there are laws against living in a public library," I say getting annoyed at the grin that is spreading across her face.

"Above the library, Sean," and then she points at the two windows on the second floor of the library.

I look up the faded red brick wall to the two windows looking out over Main Street. I can't say anything. My pulse is beating so fast. I had foolishly imagined a farmhouse or a house with a sprawling lawn. Why hadn't I even asked about this? Why didn't I go along when my parents took their trip to prepare for everything here? They invited me. They asked me if I wanted to help find a place, but I figured it didn't matter.

How could they have gotten this so wrong? I can't take it. I have to get out of here, away from my parents' eyes boring into me, waiting for my reaction. I start walking away, down the street, but that's the direction of the school, so I whip around and start the other way.

Mom grabs my arm, "Sean, talk to me, baby." I look around and see some people sitting in the café and feel like everyone is staring at the scene we are making.

I shrug off Mom's hand and begin to walk fast down the sidewalk.

"Sean," Mom yells.

"Let him go, Cheryl," Dad says quietly.

It's like I'm in some lifetime TV movie, the kind Mom loves watching. And despite my revulsion to this kind of real drama, I can feel the tears, and I start to run. Of course, just my luck, some old lady is hobbling out of the Eagle Peak Senior Citizens Center, and I almost plow her down before I turn quickly and run out into the street. I can hear Mom gasp, so I veer left and run behind a building and continue down a back alley.

I run until I am out of alleys, sidewalks, and breath. I am on the edge of town. The road winds past a decrepit metal triangular tree, then through woods, and then it turns into gravel. I keep walking toward the woods. Maybe I can find a tree to climb to get some bars.

Chapter 2: Humiliated

I am surprised by how the gravel crunches and the crickets chirp as I step outside of town limits. I stop and turn around, and there is the sign, same as the sign coming into town on the highway: Eagle Peak, Population 596. I continue my march down gravel.

We are going to live above a library. We will live above a library on Main Street. How could they? Don't they understand how not right that is?

I notice a trail leading off into a thinning area of woods with some kind of clearing beyond. I decide to take that trail into the ditch. It makes me nervous stepping on clumps of dried grass that feels kind of spongy, like there's no ground underneath my feet. Occasionally, my foot comes up a little wet, but I try not to think about it.

My anger keeps me walking through the tall grass and straggly bushes until it opens up into a sunny clearing with a little stream running through it. It's not too bad. I walk beside the water following a green leaf as it bounces over some stones that create some mini rapids. I follow it for a while until it gets wedged between two logs. I feel compelled to free it, so I bend over the water and pull it up then set it back down beyond the logs. It bounces away happily again. But as I stand straight, my right leg slips on some mud and I land hard, one leg and my ass completely soaked with mud and water. Stellar! I stand up and try to brush off some of the mud, but that just dirties my hands, so I keep walking, trying to ignore the uncomfortable feeling of wet jeans and shoes.

The trail gets more and more narrow. I'm probably going to have to turn around, but then it cuts up. I climb, and there I am on a long straight path built up. This path is easier to walk on, but it doesn't run along the stream, so it isn't quite so peaceful. I appreciate, though, that I don't need to think about where I put each step, so I pull out Trenton's playlist to drown out the endless grinding cricket sound with music. It's "Born in the USA," which is actually a good song. I keep my eyes down and step to the beat, trying to clear my mind, which drifts to Sarah and our last kiss. God, that was good. I will just go back to Minneapolis every weekend. I will bide my time here during the week and then go stay with Trenton. Sarah and I could start having sex, and then my junior year wouldn't be a complete bust.

The ground starts shaking, causing me to look up. I don't see anything, but by the time I turn, I realize I have no time to jump into the ditch and hide, which is exactly what I want to do when I see the two of them flying toward me on their oversized motorized tricycles. Within the span of two breaths, they are slowing down to pass me. The one in front, huge, muscled and blond with tan lines around his bare arms, glares at me as he passes. Why he is shirtless in this weather is beyond me, but then I notice his muscles popping out and get it. The other is a smaller version of the meathead—sensibly wearing a shirt. I immediately feel self-conscious about the mud and wetness. I pull my ear buds out, careful to keep my dirty hands hidden. The way the meathead looks as he passes is pure alpha male aggression. It's a dare, and I am in no position to take the bait, so I nod lightly and smile. I imagine Obi Wan's mind control would be useful now, a wave of the hand and a thought planted: *you don't want to talk to this strange boy. You want to keep riding your toy. You are not interested in anything here.*

Of course, that would be a movie, and this is my reality, so they don't keep riding. The meathead stops in front of me, the other a little behind me. They don't seem aware that they have surrounded me, or they don't care.

"Why are we stopping, Todd?" says the guy in back, not looking my way, just looking nervously at Todd.

Yeah, Todd, why are you stopping? Shit. I can't even walk away. There is no way I would turn my back on these guys, not with a wet ass. I just stand here like an idiot, trying to look as tough as they look. It is so not working.

"We're stopping, *Luke*," Todd says emphasizing his name like he is getting Luke back for saying his name first, "to say hello. We don't know this guy here. He's walking on our trail, and I think he must be lost. Are you lost?" he asks before he turns his eyes on me.

His dialogue sounds like a stupid '70s movie, but I don't feel comfortable as he looks at me, his eyes taking in everything from my hair down. I can tell he is particularly intrigued by my earrings, my favorite black hoops. And he pauses on my wide pounded silver ring. I consider running. They look strong, but not fast. Surely it would take them a minute to turn those massive machines around, and I doubt they would follow me along the stream path.

Instead, I try to talk. "No, I'm not lost yet. It seems a pretty clear path back to town." I point lamely toward the grain elevators.

"Does it?" Todd says, laughing a little like it is a joke.

Luke looks from Todd to me and says, "So what's your name? Are you the new kid?"

The new kid? I guess there must be only one of those per decade here. I appreciate his tone though. He is clearly attempting to be decent.

"Yeah, I guess I am. We just moved in today. My name is Sean."

"*See-On*?" Todd barks with a smirk.

"Yes, it's spelled like Sean, but it is pronounced See-an."

"Is it?" He says, again laughing like his question is funny.

Luke looks again at me quickly and says, "Come on, Todd, let's go. I'm hungry."

"Oh." Todd turns to Luke releasing all his seething anger on his friend. "You're hungry?"

Again, the repeating. It is almost funny, and yet I can't laugh because my ass is wet and I can't stop shaking. "Yeah, I should get going too," I mumble, turning to walk back to town too soon.

Todd, of course, notices my pants.

"Better change those pants, *See-on*," he says, laughing loudly. "Didn't mean to scare you."

Luke's eyes immediately search my pants, and when I look down I see the wetness has spread to the front of my pants, making it look like I pissed myself. Luke looks up at me briefly. He looks like he is in pain, but then I recognize more clearly the emotion. It is pity.

Todd revs his machine and takes off. Luke follows.

I walk back into town slowly, trying to stay off Main Street as long as possible, taking the alleys to avoid people. When I do turn back onto Main Street, I see my parents' car and now empty trailer parked right where I had left it, and they are no longer outside.

I sit down on the hood of the car, not really knowing how to go home. It seems the only entrance to the building is the library. What the hell has happened to my life? I wish the meatheads would have just kicked my ass. I would much rather have come home bloody than humiliated.

Just then an upstairs window opens, and Mom's smiling face is there. "Sean, come on up!"

"Should I jump?" I ask.

"Ha ha, no, just walk around back. There is a door and stairs," she says.

I get up from the hood of the car and walk through a narrow gap between the Eagle Peak Library and the Eagle Peak Post Office. This opens up into another alley, and around the building Mom is peeking out a door.

"What happened to your pants?" she asks, clearly more annoyed than concerned.

Better that she be mad than worried. "I sat in water."

"Okay, whatever you need to do. I'm here for you, man."

I roll my eyes. She is trying to do it again. Act cool.

"Your mom is down with your moods."

"Please, Mom," I beg, "can you just show me my room? I'm a little tired."

She looks at me more closely and sees that I am serious and leads me up the stairs, which are narrow, white, and boring.

The first room when we get into the apartment is the living room, already furnished with our couch and coffee table and lots of boxes. I feel a stab of guilt that I ditched my parents and that Mom and Dad moved all our stuff. I hadn't even asked if everything was moved in yet. What kind of son am I?

Mom says, "There was a really nice man that came out of the café to help us. Martin, I think his name was. And his son, Jasper, I think, kind of cute, had lots of curly blond hair, helped us with the big stuff."

"Sorry," I say looking down. Some stranger and their blond kid helped. Now I'm not only a pants pisser but also a slacker.

"Sorry, Schwary. You needed a little time. And just

look at the wonders that walk did for you. I've never seen you so cheery!"

"Okay, Mom," my annoyance overriding my guilt. "Can I see my room?"

She walks through the living room. To the left is the bathroom and to the right is the kitchen. It is small, but it has all the appliances and a bar thing that I assume we will be eating at.

Off the living room are two rooms and she points to my door. I walk in and close it. I don't bother looking around. There is no point. It will just suck. I walk to the bed and lay down heavily, not caring that Mom would freak about me lying on a bed with no sheets.

I look up at the ceiling and then close my eyes and tune out.

The next thing I know there is no longer any sun coming into my room and my parents are in the living room talking. I get up and grimace. My pants are still wet! Looking at my phone I see there still are no bars, so I throw it down on the bed, pull out a new pair of jeans and underwear and a clean t-shirt, and then run across the living room into the bathroom.

"He's alive!" Mom yells from the couch, and Dad chuckles beside her.

I close the door and switch on the light and look around at the bathroom. Mom already has our old shower curtain up and the shower is stocked with shampoo and soap. I tear off my clothes and jump in, happy to finally shed off that embarrassing layer of denim. After a couple minutes the water is actually hot, and I relax into the moment letting the water drip over my head. My bangs are getting long—my eyes are covered in black hair. I stay that way for a long time, just letting the hot water hit my face. After I turn off the water, I flip my head back, getting the hair out of my eyes, and then I stare at my body in the mirror. I don't have meathead Todd muscles, but I'm not a wimp either. Part of me wishes that I had spent some of the theater and dancing time in karate or something, maybe boxing, where I could have learned how to hurt someone. All I can really do is the West Side Story snapping and jazz walking as a prelude to a fight, and then I suppose I could have leaped like a gazelle into the ditch as they approached, pirouetting as I hit the trail then sashaying all the way back home.

Nope, there is no way this is going to go well.

Chapter 3: Routine

I wake up not recognizing where I am. Because this isn't the first time we moved, it's a feeling I'm used to, so I stay there remembering. I'm in my bed, in my room, above the library, on Main Street in fucking Eagle Peak. The room is large, empty, and that off-white color people think renters like. There will be no Angry Catfish Coffee and Bike Shop where my friends and I go every Saturday morning, Trenton to check out the cute barista, the rest of us to get hyper. There will be no Baker's Wife donuts that my parents will bring home hot in those little white bags. There is only silence. I lay in bed listening hard, trying to find some kind of noise. I can hear some birds, and a car drives by on Main Street just below my window, but that is all, one car and some birds. There is no hum in the distance, just the silence of my own brain reliving the memory of Luke and Todd and my hideous introduction to the locals.

I decide to get up. It's really bright. Light from the south window facing Mike's Café and light from the west, facing rooftops. I look out over the roofs of varying heights and smile. Just a step out the window and I would be walking on, what is that building—the Eagle Peak Bank? The Eagle Peak Post Office? What an odd, odd little place. I try the window and it opens easily. Later.

My boxes are sitting out on the floor, full of my music

and books. The suitcases full of clothes are lying beside the closet. I will just start organizing my stuff. Yes, that will make all the bad memories go away. Just organize and all will be well. All will be well.

I begin with my CDs. My friends mock my CD collection, the dated albums and that I even buy them. If I were really cool, I'd have a record collection, but records are my parents' thing. I pull out my CD stand, set it beside my bed on the floor, and begin to put the CDs back in, keeping them in alphabetical order by artist, then album. It is comforting to touch each case and remember better days. My Bloody Valentine "Loveless" that I found for ninety-nine cents at Cheapo, Velvet Underground Live that I bought full price, Thelonius Monk, a gift from my mother, Johnny Cash, a gag gift from my friends last year that I actually secretly enjoy.

I hear Dad get up. I know it's Dad because he always gets up first to make coffee for Mom and bring it back to bed in a cup on a plate with something sweet, usually a donut. I wonder what he will do this morning without Baker's Wife. On his way to the kitchen, he pokes his head in to say good morning, but that is it. He is about as inept as my mother before his morning coffee.

I hear him digging around through the boxes in the kitchen, swearing a little. I'm sure they didn't remember to pack the coffee pot last so it would be easy to get to.

I refocus on my CDs, quickly finishing that project. Then I move on to my clothes, shoving them onto the shelves in the closet.

By the time I am done, I can smell the coffee. It smells good, and I walk into the kitchen just as Dad is adding cream to Mom's coffee, placing it on a plate. I notice there is nothing sweet.

"Why don't you add some sugar," I suggest.

"Yeah, you're probably right," he says, and then goes into the box at the end of the counter.

I pour myself a cup of coffee too and sit down to drink it.

At last, Dad shuffles off to the bedroom with both coffees. I don't follow him. This has always been their time together in the morning, and I like my morning time too.

By the last sip of coffee, I feel my mood lightening, and it is time for my morning ritual, which always begins with My Bloody Valentine. Back in my room, I put on "Only Shallow," which begins with the four taps of the drum and then the swelling guitars, sounding like thirty of them, and then Balinda's dreamy voice. I close the shades on the window, so I can tune out Eagle Peak, and I begin to sway. I close my eyes and work into the song. I'm not worried about my parents busting in on me, for they are just as aware of my need for privacy as I am of theirs. I pick out a plain black t-shirt, a pink and green flannel shirt and some jeans—my one pair of boot cut. Shit, overalls, here I come. I'll make a little effort today to tone down my look. I even change out of my hoops for some subtle studs. I am so back to my old self by the end of the CD, I am lying on my bed thinking about sex. It is usually how my ritual ends. Today I am thinking about Sarah. She and I never had sex, but we came close a couple times, and I know she wanted to.

I open my phone and look at her last text: *I'll wait for you.* I can't believe I didn't just do it when I had the chance. If I had at least just done it, I would have some experience. I laugh out loud at that thought, for experience is definitely not what I need for this town. Girls and sex would be a lost cause here. I imagine a sea of blonde hair and blue eyes, big tits, and prep clothing. My straight friends and I made a pact to never ever date an Abercrombie girl. Maybe I should start to plan an escape weekend today.

A few minutes after the music ends, Mom sticks her head in.

"Let's go, Sean, the library is open now, and I am dying to check it out. Your dad isn't interested. He would rather head up to school. I need to go too, but I figured we could check out the library and then walk up to school together. The school is open today. There is some kind of cheerleading thing going on. Wait till you see this school!"

"Jesus, Mom, breathe," I say, already exhausted by her nerves and the idea of a school full of cheerleaders. "A little nervous?"

She sighs. "Yes."

"Okay," I mutter. "Let's just go."

I put on my black converse shoes, Mom puts on her flats, and we walk out the door. As we are walking down the long staircase, I realize Mom is wearing her favorite green shirt and some dress pants. "You look nice," I say.

"And you look like you are attempting to go country."

"Don't be mean, Mom."

And she laughs, which is the goal.

We walk around the front of our building and enter the Eagle Peak Library. I am immediately interested and impressed. I don't know what I expected, maybe a bookmobile kind of collection of books, but this is definitely beyond my expectations. In fact the library is divided in half. Half is a museum—a museum about Eagle Peak, now there's a laugh. The other half is jam-packed with books—sectioned by children, teens, reference, fiction and nonfiction. It looks like they even have a system of cataloguing.

"What?" Mom asks, not understanding my hesitance. "This is really nice!"

"Yeah, it's not exactly what I expected."

Then a scary-looking woman, red hair curled into a

tight perm, comes around the corner. "Hello," she says like a question, probably because she doesn't know us.

Mom smiles back. "Hello! We just moved in upstairs, and we came down to see this library that we've heard so much about."

Leave it to Mom. The woman's face lights up with a smile. "Oh, you are the new family in town! Working at the school, right? Is this, is this..." she pauses pointing at me.

"This is Sean," Mom smiles. "He is our son. My husband is already up at the school."

"Yes, he is the janitor, I hear."

I wince a little. "Custodian," I say. Dad has jumped down my throat about that enough for it to stick.

"Oh, yes, custodian. Sorry about that," the librarian mumbles.

"Yes," Mom interrupts. "We will all be together up at the school." She smiles at me, teasing.

"Well, that will sure be nice for all of you," says the lady, still smiling at Mom. "Oh, well, where are my manners. My name is Lucinda, and I am the librarian here. But I like to consider myself a resource beyond books. I have lived in this town my whole life. So you just let me know if there is anything at all you need."

"Well, thank you, Lucinda. We'll just look around a little today."

We begin to circle around the library. Mom, of course, is drawn to the museum area—she pauses over some old dolls, a French horn and an old petticoat in a display case. I notice the line of computers against the wall and again consider Facebooking a broadcast to my friends, but what would I say anyway? *They have a library. My life sucks.* What would Trenton make of that? I grab for my phone and realize I didn't even bring it—have I given up hope so soon? Instead I turn toward the movies. I am surprised by the selection. There are actually foreign films. Then I move on to the CDs, and I am not surprised by them—mostly country and pop. Music I won't be listening to.

I stroll around to the back of the library where the children's section is—there is a lot of noise there, mostly from a couple kids playing war. I pretend to look at a section of books, letting my eyes roll over the titles, not really seeing, as I glance to my left to where a little boy peeks around the corner holding his hands like they are a gun. His hair is a shocking red, totally unbrushed and wild. I have an urge to fall dead since I can tell by the look in his eyes that he is out for blood.

"Are you playing?" he asks conspiratorially.

I nod, humoring him, and then I duck down dramatically and look the other way to see if there is enemy sneaking in. When I look back at him with my finger over my mouth silencing to not alert the on-comers, he is gone, replaced with an older and female version of himself. She has the same flame of red hair, but it curls wildly all over the place in that uneven, messy way that makes it clear the curls are not intentional, but an unfortunate act of nature. As I stand up, I notice she is wearing bib overalls that seem to swallow her up—they are rolled up on the bottom, and under them she wears, not the tight T's I am used to seeing matched with overalls, but a sweatshirt. She is all bulk, but I can tell by the slit of a neck holding up all that crazy hair that she is tiny. I have to look down at her.

She seems to shrink. "Sorry about my brother. We were just... umm..."

I smile. "Playing war?" She blushes then and nods.

"I'll... umm... let you get back to your..." and then she looks at the shelf I am browsing and finishes, "self-help books."

I look up quickly and there is the sign, big and green. "Self Help". Jesus!

We turn away, I back to my self-help books, and her back to her game of war.

Finally, I grunt and walk away toward the front of the library where Mom is browsing the romance novels. I grab her sleeve in an attempt to pull her out the door subtly, and she follows reluctantly, but not before I hear a shriek of happiness and look to see the little red-haired boy standing with one foot on his sister who sits twitching like a freak on the floor, presumably dying. I could do better, but I assume she wouldn't want me watching that, so I keep walking toward the door.

As we are walking out of the library, Mom pauses to look at the bulletin board. "Oh, look at this, Sean! A Buddhist meeting! In Eagle Peak. It says they have them every Saturday. Oh, shoot, we missed it today!"

"Oh, shoot!" I mock her disappointment.

"Come on," she says as she pulls off the phone number and address from one of the tear tags. "You have to admit that is intriguing."

"I guess," I say, shrugging. I am used to Mom's interest in religion, but I don't really share it. Neither does Dad.

Then I notice that Lucinda is standing right behind us, ready to attack. "We have books on Buddhism if you are interested. If I remember correctly we have that one with the famous monk, um, the Dalai Lama, yes, that's it. And we have a couple on Richard Gere. I hear he is Buddhist. But if you are looking for churches in town, I can get you connected. Probably the quickest way to get on. We have the Lutheran, Methodist, and a Baptist." Lucinda stops, kind of wound up now like a toy about to be released.

Mom looks surprised, and pauses a moment. Finally she says, "No, thank you, Lucinda. That is so kind, but I think it will take us a little time to find the right place to worship." And then she stares at Lucinda, smiling relentlessly, until Lucinda finally walks away mumbling something about re-shelving.

"Well, that was awkward," I say once we are outside on Main Street.

Mom laughs.

"It's almost as if Lucinda doesn't want us going to the Buddhist meeting." I look up to my window as we walk toward the big hill.

"Yeah, I got that impression," she says. "Will you go with me? Next week? I know Dad won't."

"I don't know, Mom. Lucinda seems concerned for our souls. Maybe Dad and I should go to church," I say, still joking.

"Well, I'm going. And I think you should too. Who could have imagined there would be Buddhists in this town!"

We are walking by a "Vet's club," which seems to have nothing to do with being a veteran. The broken blinds hanging behind the faded signs of whiskey and beer look trashy. "Not me," I say. "But my guess is there aren't a lot of them."

"Yes, I get that impression."

As we climb the hill toward the school, it emerges behind the trees large and foreboding. Looking up at it like that makes it look even more like a prison, and I suppose metaphorically that is what it will be for me. Stuck in a cell with the likes of Luke and Todd and my parents eight hours a day. There will be no relief after school either. Images of Luke and Todd, Lucinda, and who knows who else bring on a new wave of desperation.

We pass the auditorium stairs that are surrounded on two sides by two huge cement pillars, and we go in the large metal doors off to the side. As soon as we walk into the building I realize what my parents find so appealing. The floors and stairs are made of some kind of shining cement with glittering pieces of colorful rocks stuck into it. Is it granite? There are stairs that lead up two flights and stairs that lead down one flight, and then I can see the curved stairs that lead to the basement from the first floor. It is absolutely huge. Mom leads the way up the two flights of stairs and down a long hallway lined with class pictures and rooms. There is nothing shocking about the hallway, but the floors and huge windows at the end of the hall make it look grander than a school. We walk halfway down the hall to the office, which looks like a typical school office, except this one has Mom's name in a nameplate on the front desk—Mrs. Anderson.

Mom notices that right away too. She walks around to the back of the desk and sits down, fingering the stapler, phone, and keyboard. I stand awkwardly in the doorway.

When the door with the clouded glass that says "Principal" opens, Mom jumps out of her seat, "Oh, Mr. Larry, I didn't know you were in. I was just giving Sean a tour of the school, and then I noticed the nameplate, and figured...."

"Oh, please sit, Cheryl." Mom stands awkwardly and I actually wonder what she is thinking. "Jim was in a bit ago and told me you were on your way, so I took the liberty of beginning to set up your desk." Mr. Larry smiles at me then and shakes my hand. "You must be Sean." He tries to pronounce my name right. "Your parents have told us all about you."

I shake his hand and try to smile, but it's weird to be on a first name basis with the principal. He lets my hand go and says, "Here, let me show your mother how to get your schedule up. Then we can print it out and you can walk around to your classrooms. If you'd like."

"Sure," I say quietly. I turn and ramble out into the hall, looking up at all the class pictures. I am in the '80s section, so there are lots of feathered hair and mullets. It's funny how all that shit comes back. I had a mullet last year, but it was just so damn ugly, even Trenton couldn't stand it. He kept saying shit like, "Nope, no party back there" when I walked by. I keep walking down the hall toward a short staircase staring at the hairstyles as they evolve into big hair, mall bangs, and then straight hair and short cropped. And then I hear some doors somewhere else in the school open and hear an annoying, but not completely unwelcome, sound—girls talking loudly, giggling, one of them kind of screaming. I realize it is coming from the hallway to my right, so I quickly back up and walk back to the office. I am so not ready for that yet.

When I get back to the office, Mr. Larry and Mom are staring at the printer, and I assume what is coming out is my schedule.

"Sean, I'm sure you are used to quite a few electives at this point, but we just tried to match your schedule from South High to our offerings here. We don't have a separate theater department, so you will be taking Junior English with all the other juniors." Not with the other sophomores? Thanks for the clarification, Mr. L. "We do have choir and band though, but I noticed you weren't in those, so I put you into advanced math as an elective. Otherwise, the other classes are pretty similar. Chemistry, Junior Government, Art, and Phys Ed."

"Phys Ed.?" I manage to choke out.

Mom smiles at Mr. Larry. "They cut our Physical Education programs in Minneapolis."

"Oh, well, that is a shame! There is nothing more important than a fit body to help the learning along."

I look at Mom, who is not holding back a smile as she looks down at the ground. "I'm sure Sean will find it a very new experience." I can tell she is about to laugh, but Mr. Larry seems unaware.

"Well, young man, here is your schedule. Why don't you two walk the halls. And if you are looking for Jim, you will probably find him orienting himself in the boiler room. That is where we keep all the janitorial goods. Oh, and you might want to check out the auditorium now before all the cheerleaders get here," he says winking at me. I have no idea what the wink means, but I am on the same page with him about that one—avoid the cheerleaders at all costs!

Mom grabs my arm and pulls me out the door. "Yes, let's go begin our tour in the auditorium."

We walk back down the hall I had just explored and down a few steps, and I stop. Unbelievable! This isn't an auditorium, it is a full-blown theater. We are standing behind the seating, which probably seats at least three hundred and fifty people, and looking up I can tell there is a huge concrete balcony over us. The lights are bright in the stage area, which is a full basketball court size. There are several heavy navy velvet curtains tucked to each side, and there is a full spectrum of lights up at the ceiling. The ceiling is a really dirty light pink and the walls are white with paintings of a little blue devil-looking fellow wielding a sword. Could that be a mascot? Turning toward the back of the theater, there is a concession stand and down some more steps the grand entryway with a chandelier and a glass case of trophies.

I finally look back at Mom, and she whispers, "I know. This sealed the deal for me."

I close my mouth, which had been open and gaping. She just smiles and pats my arm. "Let's go see the rest."

Speechless, I turn to follow Mom back out the door. As we climb the few steps back to the main hallway, I can hear more girls' voices.

"Let's go this way," Mom says, leading the way down the hallway toward the sound of squealing.

"Oh, Mom, can we please not go toward that sound?"

"What sound, Sean?" she giggles. "Could it be you are afraid of cheerleaders?"

"Yes," I answer honestly. "Particularly small town cheerleaders."

She sighs and turns around, heading up more steps. I follow quickly behind because I can hear the voices nearing. At the top of the stairs, we face two long rows of green-colored glass windows.

"Ooh, this looks fun!" She says pointing up a short stairway to a small door. It reminds me a bit of a door you would find in Wonderland, like we'll go through that door and then there'll be another smaller door and another. I realize, though, as soon as I walk through, that we had entered the balcony of the theater. The seats are concrete and cold looking, but the view of the stage from here is incredible, and I sit down for a moment to stare while Mom walks across to the other side to explore.

I could get lost in a theater like this one. I itch to be on stage doing some kind of monologue. Last year I got to state in speech for "That's Dad," a monologue that Dad had to hear over and over again. I smile remembering how it made him uncomfortable because the monologue implies the character's dad is gay, or that's what he thought. It's not like Dad's homophobic or anything, but he, I don't know, values his masculinity and thinks being gay threatens that, perhaps because Trenton is the only example of gay that he knows.

Then, too quickly to remove myself, the door to the auditorium flies open and four or five giggling girls in short blue skirts with striped blue and yellow shirts come filing in. Mom shoots me an apologetic look from across the balcony, and I get up to turn and leave.

But it is too late. "Hey! Are you guys here for the cheerleading tournament?" says the girl with curly brown hair tied up into a bouncing ponytail. Her friend with short, straight blonde hair nudges her, and says something quietly, and they both begin to laugh.

"No," Mom yells, too loud, not realizing how voices carry in a space like this. "We are the new students here. Well, he is," and she points at me.

I feel the stare of the five pairs of eyes on me then, quietly assessing the boy in the building. I raise my hand lamely, and say, "Hey."

"Heyee," says the bouncy girl. "So you're just checking everything out?" She shakes her hips while she says this, and then the girls begin to giggle again. She's gutsy, and I smile a little too because her shake reminds me of Trenton.

Then I remember Mom is watching all of this. I'm kind of mortified realizing how it will be from now on! "Yeah, well, see ya." I turn to leave.

Just then a few more girls walk into the auditorium, quieter, but wearing the same uniform.

"Just wait, we should meet properly," says bouncy, already bounding down the steps toward the seats below. And before I can run and hide, I hear her breathing heavily behind me, already in the balcony blocking the closest door out.

The girls left down on the auditorium floor are still, watching us. I turn and she holds out her hand to me, so I put my hand in hers. "Hi, I'm Jen. I'm the captain of the cheerleading squad, and probably the most in the know around here. So if there is anything you need, anything at all, you just let me know." She keeps a hold on my hand. A couple of the girls start to giggle below, so she says, "Well, I've got to get back down there. We are competing today, and we need to warm up."

Finally, she lets go of my hand. "What's your name, by the way?"

"Sean," I say quietly. My mom is with me now, which is no comfort.

"And I'm Mrs. Anderson," Mom says reaching out to

shake Jen's hand too.

"Well, nice to meet you both." She doesn't look at us though. She smiles at her friends down on the stage.

And then it just comes out. The question that has been churning in my head since she mentioned a competition. "So, Jen, what exactly happens at a cheerleading competition? I thought the whole point of cheerleading was to, you know, cheer."

I immediately regret asking this, for Jen's face falls into exasperated annoyance. "That is one thing we do, but we Rebel cheerleaders take our technique very seriously, and even though we are from such a small school, we have gone to state twice since I've been on the squad." She holds her grimace for a moment, waiting for, I don't know, an apology?

Mom jumps in. "Wow, to state twice? That must be something."

Jen's face lights up. "It was! And today is our regionals, so wish us luck."

"Good luck," I mutter, fighting back an eye roll.

Jen's eyes flick back to me, then to Mom, and then she turns around and bounces off.

We leave the theater silently, and when the door closes behind us, I mutter, "Well, that went well."

"Jeez, Sean, you and your dad are two of a kind. Have you no filters? I'm surprised you didn't make fun of the Rebels as a team name!"

I smile a little. "Thought about it." I had, but her "probably most in the know around here" was so much like the librarian's comment, it is making me think there is another ugly side of the small town business, like, I don't know, lack of privacy?

We finish our tour of the building, easily avoiding any more run-ins with cheerleaders since the school is so huge, and end up in the boiler room with Dad. He looks like he is in heaven, arranging the tools, bottles of cleaning stuff, brooms, and mops.

I hear the music start. Lots of treble and pounding bass, and I know they must be practicing a routine on the stage upstairs. Despite my revulsion to that kind of music and what they must be doing to the music, I am also drawn to watch them. I figure the whole point of cheerleading is to turn on the fans, and if these girls had made it to state twice, they probably at least have that going for them when they dance. Shaking tits and whipping hair and... I shake my head to get the thought out.

Finally, Mom and I head home, leaving Dad happily sorting.

"Well," Mom says as we walk down the long hill toward our home three blocks away. "I think we won't be seeing Dad for a bit. Should we check out the café?"

"No, please no," I say, knowing I sound whiny. "I don't think I can take any more. Can we just go home and have something there?"

Mom looks at me, and surprisingly stays quiet, and nods.

That night, after I go into my room for the night, I slide open my window that faces the rooftops. I am a little curious how challenging it would be to just step out and walk the roofs of downtown Eagle Peak. It takes me back to Mary Poppins, the play I was in as one of the main chimneysweepers. The cool breeze rushes into the room. I look down, happy there isn't a screen. The drop is far—a story I guess, what is that? Fifteen feet? Not more than three feet down and two feet across begins the next roof. Wanting a little solitary adventure, I push the window open all the way, slide through the window, and my feet find a ledge not far down. From there I am able to step across the open space and push off onto the next roof. I can still reach the window from the other side of the narrow alley, so I pull the window most of the way shut to keep out some of the cold air while I explore.

The roof is dark, and I start getting nervous again, realizing that I am walking over the Eagle Peak Post Office. I am sure that the roof won't give out on me, but I can't help imagining falling with the ceiling into a pile of letters and packages. I keep walking, bent over a little to stay hidden from someone walking by on the street below. Walking all the way across the roof, I reach a short brick wall, which separates the post office from the roof of Eagle Peak Liquor. Stepping over the brick wall, I am on a little higher roof that leads to the end of the street, and I can feel the pulsing of the country beat from below. At least I assume it is country even though now every country song sounds like pop with bad lyrics—not Johnny Cash though, he had it right. I keep walking, stepping to the beat, to the back of the building where I see the bowling alley light and laugh. All the letters are lit up except the "g" looking like "bowlin alley." That's appropriate. Really the only thing missing from this town is a southern accent.

I look down over the edge of the building into a parking lot and see some cars. One car obviously has people in it. And I can guess what is going on since the windows are fogged and there is muffled pop music playing. I lie down on the roof and look up at the sky, for the first time noticing all the stars—more stars than I have ever seen before—sharp and pointy. I stare up at them beginning to imagine Sarah and I in the car below, except I would have different music playing. Maybe Luna—something mellow but cool.

I am lost in my fantasy of a naked Sarah when someone opens a window, and the conversation from the car comes wafting up.

A girl is talking, and I sit up a little to hear better. "I

don't like this, you know, sneaking around. I don't see why we can't just go public."

I can hear a male voice mumbling something, but I can't make out the words. It must be the girl who has her window open.

"Well, you could break up with her, you know. It's not like she ever talks about you. It's like you aren't even a thing in her world. Why can't you just get over her?"

Then more mumbling and a car door opens. They are getting out, and I pull myself back down.

They are silent as they walk toward the bowlin' alley, obviously careful about no one hearing them, but not paranoid enough to think that someone might be listening to them from the roof.

I am too curious not to peek over the edge of the roof, and I see what I thought I had heard. There is bouncy Jen next to big head Todd. What are the chances of that? Barely here for twenty-four hours, and already I have dirt on two of the three kids that I know at Eagle Peak High School.

I am smiling as I walk back over the roofs to my window. I sense a new routine coming on.

Chapter 4: Don't Care

I am grimacing Monday morning when I wake up to my first day of school in Eagle Peak. This goes way beyond "jitters." I fortify myself in all black—black t-shirt, black skinny jeans, black combat boots, and black liner. Why not just shock the shit out of everyone.

I walk with my parents to school, so I'm extremely early, which is not a bad thing. I stand for a long time staring into my empty locker painted bright blue, wondering what the hell I am supposed to put there. I have never used a locker in my life, and this one even locks. At South High my locker was way at the end of the school next to the clinic that no one wants to be seen near unless you want to be pegged as pregnant or STD ridden, and our bags were searched by a security guard after going through a metal detector. But here I can hide anything in this locker. Aren't they afraid of guns or drugs in this school? I mean, I imagine more people own guns around here than in my "dangerous" neighborhood of South Minneapolis. Other kids open and shut their lockers. I can feel them looking, so I take off my backpack and coat and pull out just what I need for my first class.

Then I feel a light nudge on my side and smell a mix of flowers and something more pungent.

I'm turning when I hear, "Hi. Do you mind if I..." And there before me is one of the most beautiful faces I have ever seen in my life. I realize what she is asking, but I don't trust myself to speak yet, so I just move slightly to the side to let her through to her locker, which, incidentally, is right next to mine. I stand there, holding on to the locker door for support while I peek out the corner of my eye at her. She has blonde hair down to her shoulders, and her nose curls a little at the end, and when she brushes her hair behind her ear there is a mole right in the middle of her rosy cheek. It is gorgeous. Okay, so I am doing more than peeking. I close my mouth.

Letting her hair down again over the mole and patting it, she turns to me and smiles. "You must be Sean."

I try to smile casually. "It's Se-an. I think my parents were trying to keep up with their friend's children's names, all spelled normal but sounding different. Tanya pronounced 'Taneeya.' Monte pronounced 'Montay'," I say talking too fast.

"Oh," she says, looking around. Oh, man, TMI, TMI, TMI! Why couldn't I just say something normal? Like, yes, my name is Sean.

Looking back at me, I see her eyes for the first time and they are so dark I almost can't see where her pupil ends—the blonde hair and the dark eyes. She just stares at me. I don't say a thing, not trusting what will come out of my mouth.

"Sean," she mumbles, "is that right?"

She seems genuinely nervous as she tugs on her hair, tucking it behind her ear then patting it down again over her cheek. "Yep, that was good." I smile, feeling more comfortable with her obvious discomfort.

"My name's Lara, spelled L-A-R-A. People always get it wrong too. They want to call me Laura."

"Lara," I say wanting to add that it's a lovely name, but I don't, knowing that would be really, really creepy.

"So, you're a junior?" She asks.

"Yes, and you?"

"Yep."

We both stand there nodding and smiling, and I am sure then that she is just as interested in keeping the conversation going as I am. I rack my brain for something to say.

"This is a beautiful school," I venture.

"I guess," she says, rolling her eyes. "But when it's all you've ever known, the beauty kind of wears."

I chuckle, or I try to chuckle, casually, but it sounds more like a cackle and now I am self-conscious again. She looks around a little and I follow her eyes, noticing that our conversation seems to be causing some stares. That is when I hear his voice, throaty and unmistakable, coming nearer. "See-on," he bellows, walking past me, almost brushing against my shoulder. And then he puts one hand on Lara's stomach and whispers, "Hey fatty," then kisses her neck. I notice she moves away from his kiss and looks at me briefly, then looks down. Is that apology I see? No, what would she be apologizing about?

"Oh," she says, "Do you guys know each other?"

Todd answers, "Yeah, I met See-on. Scared the shit out of him though, huh?" and then he thumps my shoulder hard enough to hurt, and I can feel my eyes narrow. I wonder if we're going to fight and I steady myself. I've never been in a fight before, so I don't really know what to do, but I imagine balance is key.

Todd then catches Lara on her jeans loop whipping her around to face him and then laughs again. He keeps walking, allowing one hand to linger for a moment to pat her belly, like some cat parading his mouse kill before a competitor. Is this guy for real? Did he just call his girlfriend, oh, shit, I hope not girlfriend, fatty? And has she any idea that Jen and her boyfriend are fucking around behind my apartment? Just forget it, Sean. Just forget her. None of this is my life. But since when does that stop me?

"Well, he's lovely," I say, and then regret it right away.

Lara giggles tightly and slams her locker shut. It takes her a moment to compose herself, but when she looks up, she is smiling again. "See you around, Sean."

I sigh as she walks away. That, like everything else here, went nothing like I had planned. I turn to walk to my class, hoping that things will get better.

As I walk down two flights of curved stairs to chemistry, I am suddenly grateful for the time I spent in the school with my mom on Saturday. At least I look like I know where I am going, even though it is obvious as I trudge past staring student after staring student that I don't fit in. I see a couple of students texting in the sly—must be some kind of school policy against it. I want to stop and ask who their service provider is, but I know better.

Walking into the classroom, I am totally thrown off by the shelf to my immediate left that is lined with glass jars of baby animals floating in a pukey yellow liquid. I mean, yeah, I stayed away from biology anything for just this reason. I can't help it when I step back out the door, trying not to look like I am about to vomit. The baby pig is right there, the little sockets blank without the eyes.

As I stand awkwardly in the doorway, I hear the snickering begin, and then the teacher says, "You must be Mr. Anderson." It startles me, her voice, because she sounds just like the Swedish chef on The Muppets. For one irrational moment I imagine myself back at my old school where most people speak with accents different from mine. "Please come in and join us, if you will."

More snickering. No, I definitely am not at South High any more. I look out at the sea of white skin, and curious eyes, and feel my heart sink again. I recognize the girl from the library even though her bright red hair is pulled tight back into a bun and she is facing forward— one of the few not staring at me. It takes all I have to step forward into the classroom and take the nearest seat, which is unfortunately right next to the pig, floating in the jar beside me.

The lesson we are studying is scientific method, which leaves me a whole hour to think of nothing but the students' stares and all the shit I've gone through over the last three days.

When the bell rings, I shuffle out the door with the other students, most of whom are doing a very good job of ignoring me now. And then I feel a light tap on my back, so I turn and there is Luke, smiling shyly. "Hey, how's it going?" He asks.

I hope my expression doesn't look too tortured. I can't imagine why he would be treating me nicely after our last run-in. Maybe because Todd isn't around.

"Hey," I say finally. "Well, I made it to my first class."

"Yeah, Mrs. Carlson, she's kind of a bag—always giving out detention."

I'm not sure how to respond to that. I can tell Luke is really trying, but I'm not exactly interested in slamming someone I don't know, even if it is a teacher, so I just nod and start to walk away.

Luke seems to take the hint and starts walking too, letting me walk ahead of him.

I take the stairs ahead of him, knowing he's right behind me. I realize when I am out of breath on the third floor that I would actually get some exercise just walking to class. I try not to pant. And then I have another thought. Do they have any kids in wheelchairs here? I can't see how that would be possible.

English is the next class, and this time I walk in without hesitating; in fact, I get there early, so I have time to introduce myself to the teacher, who seems thrilled to have a new student. She gives me a copy of Dracula.

"Have you read this?" she asks, looking kind of worried.

"Yes," I say. Like, in ninth grade! I can't believe they are only just reading this book now! "But I really like it," I add, which I do.

I sit down at my assigned seat in back, by the window and a big poster of grammar no-nos. I am musing over the fact that every English teacher I know has some kind of poster like this hanging in their room; a lot of good they do. Most of the other students come filing in, sitting where they are used to going. I try to keep my eyes down on my book, but then I see her out of the corner of my eye and look up. I not only see Lara, but also Jen and Todd and Luke. Todd sits down in front of Lara, already leaning back to talk to her, and then he catches my eye. Not looking away, he grabs Lara's head and kisses her. She pulls way back in her seat and glares at him. I can also see Jen staring at Todd from her seat on the other side of the room. Luke keeps his eyes forward, avoiding me it seems. The redhead walks in too, talking with some blond guy, and they sit up in front, smiling at each other like there is a private joke going on. I can't really imagine a worse situation than this class, but I guess I shouldn't have expected to avoid these people—I mean there are only about forty kids in my class, so I guess I need to get used to this hell.

The minutes inch by, and I have a hard time not looking at Lara. She never looks back, but Todd takes every opportunity he can to turn around and pester his girlfriend and glare at me. When the class finally ends, Lara shoots up and bolts for the door, leaving Todd staring at her. I stand up cautiously and leave, dreading the next hour—Civics.

When I walk into class, I notice Lara right away, sitting in the back, her forehead in her hand. Jen is sitting next to her, leaning in and talking quietly, and I wonder what she is saying. I imagine she is telling lies. When she looks up and sees me staring, she taps Lara and says something, but Lara keeps her eyes down. And then, suddenly, I realize I am standing in the doorway like a moron. In that moment, I move my legs, and I decide to play the part of not caring. Why should I care? So Todd doesn't like me, Luke makes me uncomfortable, Jen is cheating with meathead Todd, and Lara is the clueless unhappy girlfriend. So what? They have nothing to do with me. All I need to do is bide my time in this hellhole. I tell myself I can go home any time and see my real friends. Feeling released from my misery, I walk confidently across the room to the teacher's desk and say, "Hi. I'm the new kid."

Mr. Rother looks up from his book and smiles absently, "Yes, Sean?"

"Yeah." I decide I am done caring whether or not people say my name right.

"Have a seat." He points at a desk in the front and then goes back to his book.

It is a fairly forgettable lecture about the legislative branch of government. The teacher is as boring as he is bored, and my notes are mostly doodles of faces and shapes. Sitting in the front row has its advantages. I have nothing to distract me, so it is easier to keep up the act of non-caring asshole. I even start to slouch in my seat and stick my legs into the aisle.

For lunch, I avoid walking into the cafeteria. I do walk by, but all I see are loads of younger kids filing through a slop line. Technically, we can go anywhere around school for lunch, and I know I would be more than welcome in the boiler room or the office, but instead I go outside and sit on the stairs to the auditorium, perched on the hill overlooking all of Eagle Peak. It is quiet here, but I am hungry, so I vow to bring something to eat from home from now on.

I pull out my phone, flip it open, and there it is. My

savior—one bar. I leap up and stretch my arm as tall as it goes and look up. Yes! Two bars. I text Trenton like that, arms raised high above my head—just one word: "Help!" Of course there isn't an exclamation point in my text message.

After a very dull Junior Math (where do they get these names), the last hideous hour of class is Phys Ed. Phys Ed., nothing like ending the day with a bang! We actually have to run two laps around the football field across the street from the school. I feel out of shape, but luckily I'm not panting like some of the poor saps. Then we play soccer. I end up on the mostly girl team because Jen and Todd are team "captains," so basically that means I am on the cheerleader team and it's a pretty even game, but I barely get the ball at all since everyone seems to avoid me. And despite losing in the last, what, inning, my team stays optimistic. Oh, if Trenton could see me now!

As I walk back to my locker, staring down at my phone with no bars among the sea of white faces, I feel more alone than ever.

The week goes on in this way. While on the auditorium pillar, I manage to text Trenton monosyllabic daily updates, like "sucks" and "laps" and "white" and "prep." He isn't responding—what, does he want me to lie? I keep up my act of not caring, and I actually start feeling like I really don't care.

Chapter 5: Getting Buddhist

The only thing that is remotely interesting is my rooftop exploration. Last night, I actually found a ladder that went down to the ground from the back of Eagle Peak Liquor, and I found a door that wasn't locked above the Eagle Peak Senior Center that led to an abandoned loft space. The room is a small box—just wood and dust—but the floor is actually warm, sucking heat from the old people below. I decide it is my official hangout. I will listen to my music and even do some homework up there using a flashlight. It's totally geeky, but it's nice to have a secret hideout.

Friday night as I am about to open my window and go out, my mom peaks into my room and says, "Don't forget about the Buddhist meeting tomorrow morning, Sean." I am glad I waited to leave through the window. I'm not worried about my mom not letting me go out exploring; I am more worried about her wanting to join me.

"Sure, Mom," I say, hoping she will be happy and leave me alone. She does. She just smiles and leaves the room, shutting the door behind her. I grab my coat and a clean sheet and slide out the window as quietly as I can.

I scale the two roof dividers to my hideout and open the door—you have to kind of lean and push on it to get it open. The floor is really dirty, so I spread out the sheet and sit on that. Then I stand up and start reciting "That's My Dad," the monologue I know so well. I'm up there for a good hour just acting out scenes, doing some mouth and face stretches and such. It feels good.

The Buddhist house doesn't really look Buddhist. I guess I expected something more different, maybe a big Buddha statue in the garden or something, but it is just this big white house with blue trim. Some gardens with dried clumps of brown plants surround the house, and there is a barn-like garage. There isn't anything, in fact, to signify that Buddhists live here.

My mom rings the doorbell, and we only have to wait a moment before the door opens and a friendly-looking woman welcomes us in.

"I'm Cheryl and this is Sean. We're the ones who called about the Buddhist meeting?"

"Yes, yes. Of course. Come on in. I'm Janine," she says, pointing to herself. "We are already chanting, so please come on in. We will begin the meeting at ten, but we usually chant an hour before," she says.

"Oh, Sean and I are just here to observe. Just do what you would usually do." My mom says. Observe? What am I going to observe? Why do I never ask these questions? It just pisses me off what my mom gets me into.

Janine turns to walk up the stairs, waving at us to follow as she disappears around the corner.

I turn a nervous face to my mom, and she gives me her cheesy smile and says quietly, "Well, let's go get Buddhist."

I love it when she is inappropriate, but I roll my eyes and follow her up the stairs. Although the outside of the house looked totally normal, I can immediately feel the difference as we enter the kitchen. First, there is the chanting, monotonous and droning, coming from the living room. Then there is the smell of burning incense, which is different than the stuff I am used to. It's not perfumey like Nag Champa; it's metallic, not earthy.

We walk into the living room, and I catch my breath, my heart sinking into my stomach. There on the floor is Lara. Lara? Yes, it is definitely Lara. She is kneeling in the middle of the living room as is some man and a woman, all of them chanting together and staring at the same wall. I sway a little as I stop, and I can't really take my eyes off of her, for she is quite honestly the last person I would have expected to see here. She is just sitting there, very still, holding some beads in her hands and chanting the words easily. I am confused, wondering if she is checking this out for the first time too, but she seems way too comfortable doing what she is doing for this to be her first time. I can't wrap my head around what she might be doing here chanting like this, and it isn't until she begins to blush a little, her cheek getting pink around her mole, that I actually make myself look away toward the wall that they are looking at.

There are three large wooden tables. The lowest table has candles, some plants, and the incense burner. The second table has some fruit, a bottle of wine, and some other small brass containers of things. Then, the highest table has a wooden box with open doors and a scroll inside, with what looks like Chinese writing, just some brush strokes on the page going up and down. I look back at everyone and they all seem to be staring at the scroll. Lara's eyes break away and she meets my gaze and smiles a little, so I try to smile back. Her eyes turn back and she continues on with the chanting.

Janine and my mom are talking quietly beside me. Janine is pointing out this and that, and then looks at me and says, "Sean, would you like a chair to sit in?"

I look at everyone else kneeling on the floor and say,

"No, I can floor it."

She indicates where we should sit down, and my mom pushes me over a little, so I am sitting very close to Lara. She looks over at me again and smiles. I try to sit like everyone else, legs bent under me, but my tight jeans make it really uncomfortable, so I push my legs out in front of me and then cross them. I am still squirming when Lara sits up a bit and taps the man that is sitting in front and points at a small stool beside him. He hands it back to Lara without looking at her, and she turns to me. She never stops chanting though as she demonstrates how to put the stool under her butt between her legs, and I just sit there and stare at her butt. It's perfect and round, and then she gives it, the stool, to me. I take it and mutter "thanks" and do as she showed me. It actually helps a lot; quite an invention, that stool.

And then the man in front rings the bell and everyone's chanting slows to a stop; they all bow down at the same time, just a slight bow, but it feels very respectful, kind of how I feel right after a good song ends. The man turns around and smiles at my mom and I. He stretches out a hand to my mom first, who shakes it eagerly, and then he shakes my hand. "I'm Gerald," he says. "We are so glad you could both make it. We were all pretty excited when we heard you would be coming." And then he smiles at Lara. I look confused at Lara and back at him.

"Forgive me," he begins again. "This is my family. My wife Janine and my daughter Lara. I think you have met in school. And this is Mabel. She is like family, but not really."

My head is spinning. Two of these Buddhists are Lara's parents? That would make Lara... Buddhist?

My mom notices my silence, and says, "Yes, Sean was nice enough to come with, but really, I was the curious one. I have been so curious about Buddhism, and I am just thrilled and amazed that it is in Eagle Peak that I actually get to learn about it!"

The meeting continues with Gerald giving an explanation of the history of Buddhism and Janine talking about Karma or something. At one point I catch her saying, "We are so programmed to believe we are the center of the universe, and while that is true, we are also one with everything else." I'm sure my mom is just eating this shit up! I tune out again. Lara is sitting right there next to me, close enough to touch. It's like there is an electrical current running between us. I don't need to look to know she is there, and I know if she got up and walked away I'd feel it. Have I ever really felt this kind of electricity with Sarah? I'm sure my mom notices my distraction, but I don't care. I just sit quietly reveling in the feeling of being near Lara.

"Well, shall we try it out?" Gerald's question shakes me out of my daze.

I look at my mom, and Janine is helping her get beads on her hand. Gerald hands a set of beads back to Lara, who holds them out to me. I reach to take them. "No, hold your hands like this," she whispers.

I hold up my hands the way she had, and she pulls the beads over the middle fingers of each hand and then lightly pushes my hands together. I just do as she shows me, not trusting myself to smile or say thanks. I feel a little pathetic—my heart hammering in my chest like a horny middle schooler. I have to get a grip!

Then Gerald rings the bell three times and everyone begins to chant again. I look over at my mom who is reading the words from Janine's book; of course she is chanting along like it was nothing abnormal. I try to catch the words, but I can't get it. A couple times I start, thinking it would be the right sound, but I am always one beat behind. Then Lara opens her book and begins pointing to the page. It turns out we are just repeating the same six sounds over and over, and that makes me feel really stupid. At last, I can say the words without looking at the book. It is trippy, but I find the melding of voices relaxing. I can't hear my own voice separate from everyone else's. I can actually feel the electric current between Lara and me expanding; I can still feel her, but I'm staring at the scroll with all the Chinese writing, and my eyes blur everything, but the scroll seems brighter. I can lose myself in all the squiggling lines, finding shapes of eyes. At one point I feel like I can see through the scroll. It is like nothing I have ever experienced before, and I feel a little disappointed when the bell rings again and everyone slows down and stops.

Gerald turns again, smiling. "Well, that is the chanting we do morning and night."

My mom gushes, "That was wonderful! Thank you so much for sharing this with us!"

Janine perks up. "You are always welcome in our home. Please let me know when you would like to come back."

I notice she says "when" and not "if."

"There are some snacks in the kitchen. Why don't we go have some coffee, Cheryl?"

My mom follows everyone else into the kitchen, and Lara and I stand up.

"So, you're... Buddhist," I say, still slightly stunned.

"Yeah, I guess I am." She looks down and brushes her bare foot over the carpeting. I look down too. Her toes are red, which I usually don't like, but against her skin it is super sexy.

"That's cool," I mutter. "I didn't know."

She grunts a little. "I guess I don't like to wear it on my forehead. Growing up, in this town with all these... Christians... I got used to being told I was going to hell, so I guess I just stopped talking about it."

"I could see that." I pause, wanting to keep the conversation going. "So my mom and I had to get through Lucinda to get to this meeting."

"Lucinda?"

I launch into the telling of our interaction with the librarian, how it was obvious she had overheard us and wanted to stop us from going to the meeting. Lara listens intently, staring at my face as I talk. The attention makes me more animated than I have been in a while, and I embellish a little, acting out the part of Lucinda, perched like an eagle ready to strike. We are both laughing when my mom and Janine come back into the room.

"Well, I should get going, Sean; your dad is probably wondering."

"Yeah," I sigh, and turn to go.

Lara reaches out to me. My heart kind of sputters, but her reach turns into a sort of wave, and then she lets her arm drop. "It was nice talking to you," she says quietly, looking down.

"Yes, this is Lara's first guest too!" Janine says enthusiastically. "What did you think, Sean?"

"It was great," I respond honestly, referring to not just the chanting.

My mom smiles, and I know by the way she looks from me to Lara that she knows exactly what I am referring to.

I'm in a haze as we walk out the door, but I notice in the dried up flower beds there are a pair of hand-painted gnomes, clearly done by a child. I smile thinking about Lara as a girl with pigtails and a white sundress on tanned shoulders hunched in concentration of each dripping paint stroke, and her parents watching with pride behind her, arms around each other. It is a nice image if not completely cheesy and pedophiley. Is that a word? Get a grip, Sean! As my mom and I turn down the alley, we have to step out of the way of a car. As it passes, I see Todd in the driver's seat alone, staring at me—eyes wide and angry. My smile fades instantly when I realize he is probably going to visit Lara, his girlfriend. I try to tell myself I don't care like I've been doing all week, but it doesn't work this time.

At home during lunch, my mom is animated as she tells Dad all about the meeting. "You should have heard them all together chanting. It was beautiful," she says.

Then she begins to chant, "Nam-myo-ho-ren-ge-kyo..."

She keeps chanting until Dad raises his eyebrows and says, "So I guess you're both Buddhist now?"

Of course my mom says, "I think I am. This is what I have been looking for. I think."

I look at Dad and roll my eyes, and I think maybe if my mom wasn't here, he would have rolled his eyes too.

I decide to take a walk around town after lunch and bring my phone, hoping. The little stream I had walked along before runs right through downtown, but here it just looks like some overgrown grassy ditch. I walk over it along Main Street and across Highway 71, then through the Lutheran Church parking lot. Big lot, empty now. I check my phone—nope, nothing new here. I walk to a gas station called "Eagle Truck Stop." I smile; nothing shocks me anymore. The windows are covered in colorful blue and yellow paint announcing the upcoming game of the Rebels. Everyone in the café is grey-haired and staring out at me, and I realize I have absolutely no place to hang out unless I want to chill with the geriatric population of Eagle Peak.

South Street West is the name of the street I turn on. I cross the stream again, the weedy ditch cutting through the park. I am tempted to go and swing, but I can't shake the feeling of being watched. Walking a few more blocks

I see that South Street West has turned into South Street East, and I shake my head. I wish Trenton was here to see this! He's the biggest smart ass in the universe.

Straight ahead at the end of this block is the woods. Then I see I am walking by Lara's house. Shit! I didn't mean to come back this way. Now she probably thinks I am stalking her. Unless, yeah, why would she be looking out her window. I casually look toward the house, and then turn away when I see her mom and dad in the yard raking.

"Hey, Sean, out for a stroll?" Her father asks. He is laughing a little. Why is he laughing at me? I just wave and keep walking.

Later I call Trenton from the concrete perch at school, the only place in town that I get a bar. We laugh about Eagle Peak, and then I share some more personal stories with him.

"What kind of hot is she, Sean?" Trenton asks.

I realize I don't know. What kind of hot is she? I decide to be honest. "Well, she has this mole on her cheek and blonde hair and really dark eyes."

"Mmhmm." Trenton sounds bored. "Doesn't sound like your type."

"What do you mean?" I ask kind of annoyed.

"I mean, it's not Sarah."

Leave it to Trenton.

That night I slide the window open quietly and shiver. A cool breeze is blowing in. I consider ditching my plans to go rooftop exploring, but it is sacred, routine.

Chapter 6: Rally

Despite my attempt to blow off people at school, the next Friday everyone seems happy and excited, and it's hard not to feel something. By the time I get to the third floor hall, I am actually smiling a little at a couple of the girls who look at me, but when I see Lara walking up to her locker in the tell-tale blue and yellow shirt and short blue skirt, I almost keep walking. A cheerleader? Seriously? She can't be! Unfortunately, I need something out of my locker, and as soon as she notices me she turns, smiling, and says, "So, are you going to the pep rally this afternoon?"

So many thoughts run through my head, so many things I want to say, like, are you kidding me? Or you do know that you look like a bumblebee, right? Or how could you possibly be so hot and Buddhist and a cheerleader? But, my mom would be proud. I filter. I say, "Um, I have never done that kind of thing before."

She laughs at me then, and says, "Jeez, Sean, you act like I am asking to do some kind of crazy twisted kinky shit with you or something. It's just a pep rally!"

And then she blushes, and oh, God, it is just too much. I think, oh, please please, please ask me to do some crazy, twisted, kinky shit with you!

"Well, it is my first," I say, actually proud of my ability to keep the sex reference alive.

"What, you didn't have pep rallies in Minneapolis?"

61

she asks, trying to seem shocked, but I can tell she is still embarrassed.

"Yes," I say slowly, still thinking about all the crazy, twisted, kinky shit I want to do to her, "but it wasn't exactly what my friends and I did, you know?"

"Well, here everyone goes, unless you want to take a voluntary study hour in the shop studio."

Well, that pretty much nails it! So to speak. "I'll be there," I say quickly. She smiles. I step back and wave theatrically at her outfit, noticing her perfectly sculpted legs. "I assume you will be there too?"

"Up on stage," she says.

Her skirt catches my eye as she fidgets. "Is that a wool and polyester blend?" Another repertoire of knowledge—thank you Trenton. I can't help but reach out and touch it. She doesn't step back, so I keep it in my hand rubbing it. "Isn't that kind of hot and uncomfortable? I mean I would have thought they would be cotton." My hand brushes against her leg, and her muscle tenses. I am definitely feeling it. Then I realize I am talking about the material type of her skirt, and it is my turn to be embarrassed. I quickly bring my hand down, but she still seems unfazed, just a little confused.

She smiles then and says, "Yes, it's hot."

"Hey, Lara, let's go." It is Jen interrupting. "Oh, hi, Sean. Are you coming to the pep rally today?"

"Wouldn't miss it for the world, Jen," I say, staring at Lara, who seems to notice my sarcasm and smiles a little before turning toward her friend. I stand there as they walk away, but people are watching me too, probably because I just had an extended interaction with the school's beautiful people.

When I find out that we won't be having gym because the pep rally is final hour, I am suddenly pleased about the whole thing. How bad could it be?

As I am herded into the auditorium, I notice Luke looking at me. Feeling bad about the earlier blow-off, I nod and wave a little. He smiles and walks over to me. It is the first time I really notice him actually. I wonder if he always has dressed like that and I had just missed it or if this is a new development. He is wearing black jeans and a black t-shirt. I haven't seen many people in all black, and I can't help wondering if I am the impetus for this style. Yeah, as if.

"So, you want to sit by us?" He waves at the rest of the guys, all obvious jocks who look irritated that I am being invited to join them. Well, what the hell, I think, I don't see Todd around.

We sit in the very back row. Behind us is a thick concrete wall that we all lean our heads on. It isn't my preferred seat.

Luke is first at starting our conversation. "Kind of lame, huh? I bet your pep rallies were a bigger deal than here."

I look around at the auditorium filled with kids, the streamers draped above us in blue and gold, and the cheerleaders all lined up on the stage/basketball court. "Nope, I am pretty sure pep rallies are a bigger deal here."

Luke looks at me like he is surprised. "Wow, they must have been pretty bad."

"Yep," I agree. Surely he wouldn't understand. Then I overhear one of the guys down the row say, "dibs on Haley", and another shouts out, "Jen," and then another, "don't mess with her, unless you like to be sloppy seconds."

"Seconds?" Someone else says, "try thirds!"

They all laugh, and Luke turns toward me. "It's kind of a game we play—which cheerleader do we want this day."

"Yeah, I kind of gathered that." I say, turning away.

"So, who do you want?" he asks quietly.

"I'm not really into cheerleaders," I say.

"Me neither," he says, beaming at me.

Fortunately, the music starts. It is Dee-Lite. Interesting choice of music—very dated. The cheerleaders are bouncing now, walking forward, getting into formation. It is embarrassing, but I can't not stare at them, especially Lara, right next to Jen in front. When she stops, just tapping her foot, her breasts keep moving under her shirt. I try to look up at her face, but then they are moving, all of them synchronous, doing moves that would be more appropriate for S&M night at a rave. Their hair, all down and around their shoulders, swirls and flips, their hips are as crazy as a belly dancer's, and the muscles in their thighs keep popping out. I can't help but imagine them holding whips and sporting fish net stockings.

I quickly gather that Lara and Jen are the flippers, which is why they are often in front, their front flips crossing each other, their splits perfectly timed slams into the wooden floor. When the music stops, the crowd is cheering, and Lara is smiling and bouncing backwards to her seat. I am silent. They are actually really good. Slutty, but good.

Luke nudges me. "I thought you didn't like cheerleaders."

I look at him and am surprised to see the dismay on his face. Exactly why is he being so friendly? I've seen this look of fear and hope in many an acquaintance before Trenton could tease me about being straight in front of them. It feels different here though. Threatening.

When Principal Larry starts talking into the microphone, I turn back to the stage, trying to keep that thought out of my head. He briefly announces that the cheerleaders are headed to state again this year, and there is a squeal on stage. Then he announces the football game that night would be the team's opportunity to go to regionals, and for that there is both squealing and loud hooting from around me. It seems I had managed to sit beside the entire football team. Even Luke is hooting and pumping up his arms. I sit a little lower in my seat as all the other kids turn around to stare at us.

Mr. Larry interrupts the elation. "But now, we have an important announcement about the game. I am sorry to say, well, Todd will not be with us tonight."

The crowd boos and hisses, and all the players around me look at each other.

"Wait, wait. Todd's grandfather will be filling in for Todd, so we don't need to worry."

"What the fuck?" one of the guys says out loud.

A murmur goes through the crowd as the back door to the basketball court opens, and in walks a very large but bent over old man with a cane. He walks very slowly across the court, nearly tripping a few times, but as he comes closer, I see that it isn't an old man. It is Todd wonderfully made up with a crazy grey wig, thick glasses, and lots of layers of ill-fitting clothes, his pants pulled up to his chest. I lean way forward in my chair wondering what the hell is going on. I am not concerned at all about the football team. My concern is only that my idea of Todd is way off; the way he carries his body and holds his face in that old man scowl is brilliant. And given that there is no form of theater instruction for at least a hundred mile radius, it means he has raw talent. I can't take my eyes off of him.

He hobbles to the podium, and just as he painstakingly pulls out the microphone and brings it to his mouth, the music comes on, loud and pumping, and he throws the mic stand to the floor. No one in the whole auditorium speaks or whispers. He has us exactly where he wants us.

And then he is moving with the music. First like an

old man, keeping the scowl on his face like he is really concentrating. His hips pump spastically side to side, and that is when people start to laugh. When his hands move up to his chest and begin unbuttoning, the crowd erupts with cheers. And I watch in horror as Big head Todd strips down to shorts and a t-shirt, brilliantly changing his style of dance with each layer he takes off. By the end of the whole thing, most of the students are standing and cheering wildly. The hooting around me is deafening. I stand only to see, but I do clap. It was brilliant, and I would be a total ass to not give him that.

The rest of the pep rally goes by quickly. Todd takes his throne up on stage with all the cheerleaders, and after the coach gives his boring speech, they get back up and do another routine, Todd right in the middle of it, standing there swaying comfortably, and in the end he catches Jen in his arms as she flips off the top of the pyramid. Lara is on the bottom, feet wide, bracing two girls above her with her strong arms, and as they push off and jump from her shoulders, her smile never moves. She is amazing, so controlled. It reminds me of her kneeling and chanting, totally focused.

When it is all over, I sit and watch as Luke walks up onto the stage and hits Todd on the back. Todd turns, smiling, and hits him on the shoulder. They start talking and Lara walks over to them. Jen intercepts Lara, though, and pulls her toward the door. I get up to leave too. As I walk out of the auditorium, some of the jocks manage to smile a little at me. And I try to smile back. Overall, it was a very odd, creepy, and kind of exciting experience. I feel like I am losing it. Do I really feel peppy after going to a pep rally?

Chapter 7: A Little Lame

I must be quite altered by the pep rally, because after school that day, I find myself walking down to the boiler room to find Dad. I feel like talking with someone, and I know my mom will be busy for a while. He is just leaving to clean out the classrooms since most of the students are gone. I help him carry the big garbage bin up the first level of stairs.

"How do you do this when I'm not here?" I ask a little out of breath.

"With these bad boys," he says, flexing his muscles.

I stand staring at my father, painfully aware of the few students who are down the hall looking at us. "You were a jock, weren't you?"

He laughs a little. "Nah. I did play sports, but I was kind of quiet."

"That doesn't mean you weren't a jock, Dad."

"I was me. Why do you feel this need to classify everything?"

"Oh, just forget it," I say, starting to roll the garbage down the hall.

I watch as my father goes into classroom after classroom, pulling out the garbage, wiping down the boards, and straightening the desks. He works quietly and quickly, and I can tell he just wants to get done with this part of his job. I roll the garbage behind him throughout the whole building and carry it up the flights of stairs.

We don't talk much, but I am able to listen in on some of the teachers gossiping with each other or talking on their phones in their rooms. It is interesting how their whole demeanor changes when there aren't students around. My father and I don't matter much; they don't seem to be censoring anything for us. They talk openly about other students, the pep rally, their own families, their cars, and whatever else.

When I mention this to my father, he says, "That is why I call myself a transparent maintenance technician." He laughs a little, and I am sure this is a joke that he had been working on for days, just hoping for the right set-up. I just stare at him blankly but keep following.

The whole thing ends with us back in the basement. Dad promises he won't be much longer, so I sit on the floor, watching him as he bangs and swears at the huge boiler he is trying to drain. "It's like they have never drained this thing! Do they have any idea how dangerous that is?"

Of course he doesn't expect an answer, for my knowledge of the mechanical world, well, doesn't exist. I can listen though. And there is something comforting in the way he looks both annoyed and at peace at the same time.

And then I hear it. "Flaming Lips." It is music to my ears. And it comes from somewhere up in the school.

"I guess there's some kind of cheerleading practice or something," Dad guesses. Dad's knowledge of music is about as extensive as my knowledge of boiler systems, and I know that he is wrong. There is no possible way that the cheerleaders at this school would be working up a routine to this band.

"I'm gonna go have a look," I say getting up.

Dad smiles. "I didn't think cheerleaders were your type."

"That's not cheerleading music, Dad. I like this song."

"Okay. You go have a look then," he says, still smiling.

I am already out the door, turning right down the narrow hallway. I walk up the two-story staircase that leads to the main level of the school and quietly by the auditorium door, hearing that the heavy base drum and lilting guitar music is clearly coming from there. I know if I open that door I will be discovered, and I want to find out who is playing this music without drawing attention to myself. And then the music stops, and I freeze, worried someone will come out and see me stalking.

I stand for at least a minute, and then it is back, the distorted beginning of "Watching the Planets", and I run down the hall, down a few stairs to where the door to the seating in the auditorium was left open. This is too easy. I kneel down before going through the door and begin to crawl behind the back seats until there is a gap in the rows. I would feel like James Bond if I weren't such a creeper, but wait, JB is a creeper! This revelation gives me the guts to peak around the corner and watch.

It is beyond breathtaking. There she is in the middle of the stage, dancing—Lara, in the bee costume. Her hips and her shoulders work against each other erratically as she pops, and then she punches and kicks her legs, splitting in the air. She begins to flip over and over front flip front flip and then the splits, slamming hard to the ground and then she turns onto her back punching up again to the rhythm of the base drum. And as she does this, she scoots her feet up behind her back, pushing up the small of her back until she is up on all fours in some kind of weird inverted yoga move. And then a back flip up to stand where she continues on with the frantic movements of someone possessed. The way she dances is exactly how I imagine someone should dance to this song. It is so pure, so real, that I feel tears in my eyes.

Just as quickly as it all began, it is over, and she bends over her legs, breathing heavily and staring off in the other direction of the audience. I am grateful she doesn't look at me because there is no way I can look away. She just looks out, and no other song comes on. And then I hear it. It sounds like a sob, but it can't be. I listen harder, crawling forward a little, making myself way too easily visible if she happens to turn a little my way. Yes, there it is again, a sniffle, and then a groan, and then she is sitting with her head on her knees rocking back and forth mumbling something I can't decipher. Actually, no, I do know what she is saying. She is chanting. I am so thrilled with the revelation that I almost start chanting with her. That is when I start to feel bad, like I shouldn't be here watching this.

I duck back behind the seats and sit very still, listening to her chant and sob, feeling like a total schmuck, as my mother would say. I want to go up there, give her a hug or something. Or something. But then she would know that I saw everything, and I don't think she wants that.

A few very awkward minutes later, I hear a door open somewhere in the school, and I pray it isn't Dad looking for me. I imagine him calling my name, coming into the auditorium. I decide I will stay hidden even if he does. My mind is racing with excuses—*Oh, hey, I found it, my earring*, or *golly dad, you should really clean these floors*, or *hey, man, that was a good nap, did I miss anything?* Then I hear girls' voices.

"Hey, Lara, you're early!" It is Jen. Then I remember the game.

"Yeah," says Lara, her voice a little husky, "just warming up."

Jen doesn't seem to notice anything different about Lara, or doesn't care. "Hey, you guys, let's go down to the guys' locker room and decorate before we do a run-through."

The chattering girls exit the room, and I can hear Lara sigh loudly, walk across the stage, and out the door.

By the time I get home, I am totally wacked out. I am actually hopeful that the crying means Lara is breaking up with or broke up with Todd. At the same time, I feel like a total ass, spying on Lara like that and hoping I know why she is crying.

"Spill it, Sean," my mom says as soon as I walk into the living room.

"It's nothing."

"Was it the pep rally? I thought that was pretty impressive actually."

She isn't helping at all. "It's nothing, Mom," I insist, "and yes, the pep rally was impressive."

"So it was the pep rally that got you all lathered up," she smiles like she's the shit.

"Lathered up? Whatever, Mom, just lay off, okay?" I don't like to be rude, but she started it.

"Okay, okay. I know you're annoyed when you tell me to go whatever myself."

"I didn't say..." I start.

"Whatever, Sean, just relax. Let's cook dinner. How about fettuccini Alfredo with shrimp scampi?"

"Okay." I slump down on the kitchen stool.

Before long she has me chopping garlic and grating cheese. She lets me drink a small glass of wine while we cook. Trenton always talks about how cool my parents are that they let me drink once in a while with them in the house. I tell him that they do this to prohibit me from being one of the cool people, drunk at a party. Trenton, who rarely misses an opportunity to get drunk at a party, said, "Ah, it's overrated. I usually just end up messing around with someone and regretting it anyway. At least at home, there's no temptation." I miss Trenton now and decide to bring up a trip back to Minneapolis.

"Sure. We can go to Minneapolis for the next break," my mom says.

"I didn't mean we, Mom, and I'd kind of like to go before Thanksgiving!" Doesn't she understand the urgency here?

"You want to drive all the way to Minneapolis and stay overnight all by yourself?"

"Yes," I say, trying to look serious and adult-like, even though I want to giggle.

"I'll talk to Dad about it." And that is it. I will just have to wait for the verdict to come in.

Dinner is good. I am hungry, and it is my favorite meal. Then Dad brings up the game.

"Oh, that would be great, honey!" My mom practically squeals and grabs Dad's hand. "A small town football game. Can we make out in the bleachers like we used to do?"

"Mom? I'm right here, you know. That's just gross!" As much as I appreciate that my parents aren't divorced and pitting me against each other, like so many of my friends have to put up with, I don't think they need to be quite so horny.

Dad turns to me and asks, "So, you want to go?" He sounds almost, I don't know, eager. "Wouldn't that be a first for you?"

"I guess I'm into firsts here. Besides, what else am I going to do besides climb the roofs?"? Damn, that was stupid. I can't believe I let it slip like that.

"I told you," my mom says to Dad. He just smiles. "When will you take us out with you?"

"Why do you think I never told you?" I ask, getting up. They both start laughing, and my mom goes and sits on Dad's lap and kisses him. I leave, feeling lonely.

Chapter 8: Gravel

Not at all shocking, I am alone at the game too. It has that same nervous excitement that there was at the pep rally. I haven't felt that since the last rave, and it feels kind of good. I am glad that I am actually wearing something dressier. Even though everyone around me is wearing blue and gold shirts, jeans and tennis shoes, I feel very comfortable in my green plaid suit jacket over my T-shirt and black combat boots. My parents keep their promise and sit in the top of the cold metal bleachers holding hands. The cold, their loviness, and the marching band sitting in front of them keep me away and pacing along the side of the field.

Did I say band? Yeah, as if. Two flutes, one of whom I notice is the red head from the library, one clarinet, three trumpets, a couple trombones and a shit load of drummers (who can't keep time) attempt to play Queen's "We Will Rock You." And it is laughable. I try not to look at Lara too, but that takes a lot of effort because she is so gorgeous. Instead, I try to focus on the game, Luke in particular. He all but beams when he sees me and waves practically every time he comes to the sideline, which is a little weird but at least gives me something to notice. I nod my head and smile back.

Todd is the star of the show. Every catch or tackle he makes is cheered on wildly. At one point he drops the ball while he is running and the crowd is quiet. Some guy in a shiny, grey suit swears loudly. "What the fuck, Todd!" His words are slurred, but they echo above the silence. He stands out—the slick suit and the swearing.

I see Lara glaring at the man and then she yells, "Let's go, Todd!" and then she starts a snazzy cheer that spells out "let's go." They leave out the apostrophe though, and this makes me smile until I look at the suit guy who swore and see him swaying, his friends trying to hold him up. Drunk assholes exist everywhere, I guess.

Then the cheering heightens and I am looking back at the chaos of the game. I know enough about football to see that the same kids play the whole game, whether they are catching the damn ball or knocking some poor jock over, and then it occurs to me that they probably don't even have enough players to have kids sit out. Another reality of my hickville hell.

Eventually, I give up trying to make sense out of the game and watch the cheerleaders. For the rest of the game I am thinking myself out of a hard on. The way Lara smiles, that mole, her breasts bouncing as they take the field for the "halftime" show, is intoxicating. I have it bad. I've got to get a grip.

The game ends to yelling and screaming, clapping and some kind of distorted march from the band, which comes off as screeching chaos. *Hurray! We won!!!* I cheer sarcastically within.

I am waiting for my parents by the car when some kids I recognize as fellow juniors in my classes, again including the redhead, walk over to the car next to mine and, shockingly, start talking to me.

A guy holding a trumpet says, "Hey, I'm Dan. We... Jasper, Michelle, and Lindsey are going to the ditch party. Are you going? I mean, did you know about it?"

"Jesus, Dan," Lindsey rolls her eyes and stares right at me. "What he means is Hi, I'm Dan, and this is Jasper,

Michelle, and Lindsey," she says pointing to herself. "Welcome to Eagle Peak."

I smile. "Thanks, yeah, I'm Sean." I say my name right.

"We know. So, do you want to go to the party with us?" Lindsey is clearly the bold one in the group. Michelle, who is holding a flute, her red hair straightened unsuccessfully, peers at me shyly, and Jasper is dragging his Vans on the ground making circles in the dust.

"I have no idea what a 'ditch party' is," I say finally.

They laugh a little.

Dan answers my question. "It's a party. In a ditch."

"So you party by the side of the road?"

"Yep. Wanna come?" Lindsey asks.

"I... sure. Just let me tell my parents. They should be here soon."

"So what did you think of the game?" Lindsey asks.

"It was fine," and then I see them all smile like they don't believe me or something, so I fess up. "Actually, games kind of suck. I'm not a football fan. Just not my thing."

Michelle beams. "Us too. We just do it to play and entertain."

I don't know how to respond to that. They sucked so bad, and her eyes are all big, all of her awkwardness gone.

"Well, some of us do," Jasper says quietly. "I just do it to get into Michelle's pants."

Faster than I can respond, Michelle wails on Jasper and then starts frenching him. The transition from abuse to kissing is abrupt, but Jasper seems to be enjoying himself. What am I doing here watching some sadistic teen romance? When she pulls away, Jasper puts up his arms and smiles knowingly at me.

And I realize I know nothing about these kids and that they are interesting. Soon, my parents walk up, hand in hand.

"I'm going to a party tonight," I say quickly, hoping to curb further conversation with them about it.

My mom beams looking over at what she probably sees as the ideal friends—band geeks. "Well, great! Jasper, is it?"

Jasper smiles a little. "Hi, Mrs. Anderson."

My mom beams. "Thanks again for all the help unloading!"

This could go on and on, so I say, "I'll be riding with them."

Dan speaks up. "Yep."

"Okay, have a great time," my mom says stepping close to me. Then she says softly, "Don't drink too much, okay?"

In the car, I am wedged in the back seat between Michelle and Jasper. Jasper says, "Too much? She said 'too much,' like she knew you would be drinking."

"Yes, she knows. She lets me drink at home too. It's all part of her plan to keep me under control, I think. She like thinks I won't rebel or something."

"Does it work?" Michelle asks, glancing at me sideways.

I'm not sure how to answer that, so I just smile. "So, do you guys provide the music at these parties?" I ask. Totally lame joke, but Michelle still has her flute on her lap, and most people put away their instruments.

They laugh. "You're funny," says Lindsey. "And correct, almost. The kind of music Michelle plays is too risqué for the likes of that party, but she will be part of our warm-up."

"Warm up?" And my mind flashes to various horrors, and for the first time I am nervous. Are these psycho killer kids, luring me to my death? Risqué flute music? Who are these people?

We're pretty quiet until we pull off the side of the road

to what I recognize as the gravel mountains outside of town. "This is our pre-party stop," Dan says, "or 'warm-up' as Lindsey likes to say." And then he reaches over and starts frenching her in the front seat, and I'm thinking, awkward!

Michelle squeals, and yells, "Shit, guys, save it for after the party. You are scaring the new kid."

And I think, these guys are crazy and kind of cool, and they are making me nervous, and I like it.

They all get out of the car. Dan opens the trunk and pulls out a six-pack of beer—cans, which my father claims is always bad beer. Then they go running, the girls screaming, up the huge gravel hill. They look totally ridiculous trying to climb up because with every step, they slide back down yelling shit and laughing. They remind me of gerbils in one of those wheels going nowhere, especially Michelle who is doing this while holding her flute up. I can't bring myself to do what they are doing. It isn't until they are all finally at the top, laughing and teasing me, that I take a run and begin to fall up the small mountain. The gravel scratches my hands and disappears beneath my feet, so I find myself clawing and scraping up the whole hill. I am red-faced and totally out of breath by the time I get to the top, and everyone else is just staring, trying not to laugh, but when I start to laugh, everyone else does, and I realize how much I have missed this—being laughed at.

Dan is insistent that we get equal shares of beer, minus himself of course, so I get exactly one and a half beers. After each lukewarm, nasty sip, we have to say something about ourselves. It's some weird game called "truth or truth" where you have to say something true that no one else knows.

"Truth or dare is so overrated, especially when you already have no boundaries," Michelle says.

"The girls just like us to tell our inner-most feelings," says Dan, rolling his eyes.

Lindsey hits Dan lightly. "It's tradition," she says and then grabs his hand.

When it is my turn for truth or truth, I tell them random things about growing up in Minneapolis that I think they would like. And they do. They can't believe I went to my first live concert in downtown Minneapolis at the age of thirteen on a fake ID, that my friends and I go to raves, and that I have friends who were from Africa, who are gay, and who speak other languages. It is entertaining to watch them try to get their heads around what my life must have been like. They share things about school, about growing up here, lots of mention about a gravel pit, lots of inside jokes and places I don't know.

"So you must find it pretty lame here," Jasper says after a while.

"Not as lame as you might think," I say, thinking about the roofs, Lara, and Buddhist chanting. None of which I plan to share with them, at least not tonight.

Michelle clears her throat then jumps up. She starts playing her flute with a really loud high note, holding it a long time. It is painful. Then she slides down to other notes, and I quickly realize she is really good. I look at Lindsey and she just nods and smiles at me. Michelle starts to do this hip shaking thing as the main melody of Pixies' "Where is My Mind" emerges. I just stare in awe at her—she looks good like this, buried in a blue and yellow Rebels hoodie, dancing around with her flute under her pouty lip. But then I notice Jasper watching me watch her, and I look away.

Michelle finishes, and bows, smiling shyly. Lindsey and Jasper and I clap, and she looks really uncomfortable. Dan stands up. "Time to go. Let's go ditchin'!"

Everyone else stands, saying "woohoo" and then begin

to slide down the hill. I stand up and feel very dizzy. I take one step down and then fall the rest of the way, landing in a hump at the bottom. I look down at my hands and in the dim light from the highway I see lots of tiny scrapes. "I'm bleeding." This time no one tries not to laugh.

I find myself laughing with them, wondering if we really need to go to this party anyway. I almost say something, but they are in the car in a heartbeat, and Queens of the Stone Age is blaring out the open window. I figure if I had to report to Joseph Campbell, one of my mom's heroes, this would be my bliss. I sit smiling out the window stuck between the door and Michelle. I notice that rather than the flute, Jasper's hand is in her lap and that he is kissing her neck. I lean further over onto the door, watching road fly by as we speed over gravel, heading further away from Eagle Peak.

Chapter 9: Ditch

Before we stop, I notice the cars, all parked in a line along the road. We park behind the last car and walk toward the noise. It is a mixture of loud music and girls and boys yelling "chug chug chug."

When we turn and see the gathering, it reminds me of something from a movie I had seen a long time ago with my parents: Animal House. Obnoxious, drunk girls and boys slithering around like snakes, flirting with each other, and jocks lightly hitting each other. All the cheerleaders and football players seem to be here. I see Lara sitting on a log next to a dancing Jen. Lara is watching her friend, kind of quiet. Todd is one of the kids yelling "chug, chug, chug," and Luke has the end of a rubber tube sticking into his mouth, gulping down as much beer as he can, letting some of it wash down over his chin. The whole thing seems surreal. No one notices Michelle, Jasper, Dan or Lindsey, who are walking ahead of me, but when they see me, conversations and voices quiet. I feel more uncomfortable here than I do in school. There is something neutral about school, and whether I like it or not, it is comforting to know my parents are always there.

Michelle stops by the fire and starts swaying to the music, and I wonder if maybe she's a little drunk. Katy Perry is moaning about fireworks with an old time house beat. Jasper hangs back with Dan and Lindsey. I can tell they are proud of Michelle, but they aren't the dancing types. I really want to dance, but I feel like I don't even know how to move with this music. Michelle doesn't seem to care though; she just sways to her own music. I take a step out and then catch Lara's eyes. She smiles at me, a really nice smile, and I take another step. Then I'm being pulled out to dance near the fire by Jen, who is doing some obnoxious bouncing shaking thing, slamming down on each bass beat. Is it a routine?

Michelle looks at me then and smiles, grabs my hand and turns me under her arm. I like how she draws me in, so I grab her around the waist and circle her around ignoring the beat along with her. I spin her out then back, and we are right up to each other. I pull her close and feel her small waist under her sweatshirt, and I wonder what she would look like without the layers of clothing. Then I remember Jasper and back away. We both just keep swaying, and pretty soon we are surrounded by girls too drunk to stand still moving along with us. Lara watches me, well, I think it's me she watches. I miss Trenton now, again, but I feel like he might actually like this scene.

As we dance, I notice Todd walk over to Lara. He sits down next to her on the log, but then she pushes him away. They are talking quietly, staring at each other. They both look pissed. Jen bounces over to them and says something. They both stare silently at Jen until she leaves and then Lara gets up to go, but Todd grabs her arm. I'm not dancing now; I am ready to fight. But then it's over. Lara pulls away and walks, and Todd stalks off the other way. I am ready to follow Lara, but then Jasper comes into the dance circle and says something to Michelle. She shrugs and follows him, and I go too. I'd rather dance with Lara watching me, but instead I follow the four of them to the keg. Jasper and Dan get beers for Michelle and Lindsey, and that leaves me, the fifth wheel, to get my own. Luke, who is standing with all the football players, notices me and quickly grabs a plastic cup of beer and stumbles over to me, spilling some beer on my boots. I notice he isn't wearing black tonight, just jeans and tennis shoes. He wants to fit in.

"Sorry," he mumbles, wavering a little.

I put a hand under his elbow trying to steady him. "That's okay. Thanks for the beer." I take a sip and cringe. It is watery and really cold, nothing like the beer Dad shares with me.

"So you made it here. Who'd you come with?" he asks, looking serious all of a sudden and stepping closer, too close.

"Dan and his crew," I say, stepping away.

That is when Todd notices. "Well, if it isn't See-on! Luke, your boyfriend's here!"

I tense up and decide to just wait.

Luke, however, has a response, "Naw, Todd, I only have eyes for you, man."

I am both impressed and nervous. I didn't know Luke had it in him.

Todd walks directly in front of Luke, and all I see is his fist moving really fast at Luke's face. Luke's head bounces back and then forward again unnaturally and he crumples to the ground.

"What the fuck?" is all I can muster.

"You want some too, faggot?"

And then my voice comes back. "Are you referring to your fist or your dick, Todd?"

As soon as I say it, I know it is a mistake. Todd's eyes are swimming in fury. It is slow motion watching his balled-up fist come closer and closer. I throw up my hands to block it but his fist is like a fucking bullet and pushes my own hand right into my nose and eye. It's immediate pain, sharp crunching pain, and I try to hit back as Todd falls into me. I flail both arms and out of sheer luck strike flesh and hear a rather satisfying thunk, but then there is pain in my wrist. I am in so much pain that tears are falling down my cheeks.

Whatever I did to Todd seems to have worked because he's kind of staggering back, holding his throat. I bend down to look closer at Luke who is lying on his side.

"You asshole, I'm gonna get you," Todd chokes out. I tighten everywhere and stare up into Todd's eyes, which are wet and unfocused.

Then there are feet in front of me, and I hear Michelle's voice. "Fuck off, Todd!" It comes off as a kind of squeak, but I have the idea that it isn't fear but rage that is bringing out this unexpected emotion in her.

"Well, if it isn't the ag queen sticking up for the fag queen!" Todd bellows.

By then, however, Todd's reinforcements are beside him, holding him back. "Think about the team, Todd. If you kick his ass more, he's gonna go tell mommy and daddy and then you'll be off the team for the season. We need you, man," says reinforcement one.

Of course, his pleas work and Todd turns and stomps off over a little hill with a trail of believers following, Jen and her bouncing pony tail at the rear.

Dan and Jasper are by my side now, helping me stand up. Lara is there too.

"Jesus, are you okay?" she asks, slurring a little.

"No, it hurts like hell." When I bring my hand down from my nose and see the blood, I add, "and I'm bleeding."

"I'm so sorry he did that. He's an asshole."

"Then why are you apologizing for him?" I say angrily.

She looks down shaking her head back and forth. "I don't know. I really don't."

Luke groans as he stands. "Shit, Sean, he got you worse, huh? But you didn't go down like a complete loser."

I try to smile. "Well, I didn't just drink half the keg. That'll kill you, you know."

He smiles a little. "We should probably go. He'll be back."

Lara frowns. "I'm leaving too. You want me to drive you two home? Luke, you drove, right?"

I notice then she is weaving too, and say, "Why don't I drive? You don't look entirely with it either."

Dan says, "Are you sure? You look pretty bad."

"Yeah, I'm fine, and I haven't been drinking much, which leaves only the two of us to get everyone home."

I look at Michelle, who is still looking off where Todd disappeared like she is standing guard or something. I want to thank her, but it's complicated. I'm relieved, but also really I'm kind of pissed that she got between Todd and I, obviously thinking I couldn't take care of myself. She's like half the size of me and fierce as hell.

"Okay," Dan finally says.

Jasper says, "Sorry it went down this way."

"Me too," I whisper, trying to keep the tears at bay, which is hard because every nerve in my eyes is stinging.

Luke lets Lara get in the front seat, and he slumps down in the back. He is quiet, really quiet. Lara and I are too.

I start to drive toward what I assume is Eagle Peak, Lara finally says, "Take a left here. It'll take you to 71, take a right and that will get you back to town." She sounds completely sober now.

"You okay?" I ask glancing over at her.

"Yeah, I'm fine," Lara says, sill staring out the window.

"He loves you, you know," Luke says quietly from the backseat.

I struggle not to swerve off the road at that comment; instead I cough. How could he know? Why did he say that?

But instead of the laughter I half expect from Lara, she whips around and glares at Luke. "What do you know about it?" she yells. "Does he show his love for me by screwing Jen?"

My mind is reeling. I am part relieved that this conversation isn't about me and half shocked that she knows about Jen.

Luke seems to wonder the same thing. "You know?"

And this is the wrong thing to say. Lara starts screaming and stamping her feet and I try to look at the road and not stare at the tripped out Buddhist cheerleader freaking out beside me, but I keep looking over at her. And then she is calm and there are just tears. "How can you not have told me, Luke? We've been friends for like forever. You've always trusted me..." she drifts off and just stares out the window again.

It is quiet now, and I feel so outside of everything.

Everyone has all this history, and here I am in the middle of it all.

I drive to Lara's house because I don't know where Luke lives. We stop in the driveway. She turns in her seat and grabs Luke's knee. "It's okay. I know how he is. It's hard not to want to protect him, but we can stop. He's not a kid anymore, and he can take care of himself. We're okay, right?"

It's so intense. I feel like I shouldn't be here.

"Yeah, it's okay. I'm sorry, Lara," Luke says. He sounds so sincere. I just look ahead.

"Sorry for all the drama tonight, Sean," Lara says and her hand brushes my arm. I am annoyed that my arm gets goosebumps where she touches.

She gets out of the car and shuts the door. Yeah, no problem, any time, I think. I sit in her driveway until she is at her door, and as she opens it, she looks back at the car and gives me the saddest look ever, waving a little—it reminds me of when she reached out to touch me after the Buddhist meeting, and I feel shivers run down my legs, wishing like always that things had gone differently.

After sitting in her driveway for a minute, Luke finally catches on. "Oh, yeah, you don't know where I live. Just drive to school. I'm right across the street from the ag addition."

"Okay," I say, thinking about my earlier naivety that future farmers would be my main source of discomfort in this hellhole.

When I stop Luke's car in his driveway, I get out and wait for Luke to pull himself out.

He walks slowly around the car, looking like Todd had kicked every bone in his body. I recognize the feeling though. I, too, feel numb with pain.

"I'm sorry, Sean," he says.

"Why do you people apologize for him?"

"It's not just for him. I mean, it is, but I'm sorry for Lara too. She's a good friend and I should have told her about Jen."

Yeah, me too.

"Lara's the only one who's understood me, you know?" he asks.

"No," I say. "I don't know anything about anything, Luke."

"And Todd, he's been my friend forever, you know. He's not all bad. His dad's a real asshole. Todd doesn't mean to be."

The string of excuses is making me sick. "I gotta get home, Luke."

Luke steps closer. I stand my ground and look down at him. He grabs my hand and when I try to pull away, he leans in like he is going to kiss me. Shit, even his eyes are closing.

"Luke, no," I say, forcing my hand out of his tight grip.

"But..." he says trying to grab my hand again.

It is so pitiful, his desperate grab into the air, his inability to say something.

"Luke, you're drunk. Go to bed," I say, starting to walk away. "I'll see you later, okay?"

Walking a few more steps, I turn to see Luke staring after me. He looks completely stunned, and I feel bad, so bad, that I have caused him even more pain on a shitty night like tonight.

I keep walking though, down the hill, back to the library, up the stairs, across the living room, which is dimly lit by a night-light, and into the bathroom. I avoid looking in the mirror as I walk in, use the toilet, and then splash water on my face. But when the sting of the water hits my eyes, I look up and gasp. My nose has dried blood all around the nostrils, my right eye is completely bloodshot, and my face is already puffy between my eyes. I imagine that the hunchback of Notre Dame must have looked something like this, and I wonder at Luke even wanting to kiss this. Walking through the kitchen, I grab some frozen peas and crash on my bed, gently placing the ice-cold bag on my eyes and nose, hoping that will take care of the swelling. It works in the movies, anyway.

Chapter 10: Wince

I wake up the next morning feeling like I have survived two tons of gravel being poured over my head. My hair is soaked from the bag of frozen peas that have thawed overnight. Slowly, I try to open my eyes, but only the left one opens. The right eye won't open no matter how much I will it to, and I can't help but reach up and touch it. The pain of my own finger causes me to sit straight up in bed and swear loudly, despite my intention to keep quiet.

My mother comes running into the room. "What, what, See-see," and then she sees me. "Oh, my God, what happened to you?" She almost looks like she is going to beat me up for getting my ass kicked, and I flinch a little.

Then she softens and smiles. "Oh, baby. The party didn't go so good?"

I look up and can't believe she is trying to make a joke.

She sits on my bed then and grabs my hand, noticing the scrapes on the palms and even the knuckles from the climb and fall on the gravel. "Does this mean you got the jerk back?"

"How do you know I'm not the jerk, Mom?" And truly, thinking about Luke and that look on his face makes me feel like a total asshole. I know that what Todd did to him was nothing compared to what it must feel like to try to come out of the closet and then be denied. And then I am mad because, like everyone else, I am making

Todd out to be less of an asshole than he really is.

"I know you, Sean. You don't fight."

I lay back down, turning away from her. I feel horrible, and talking to my mother about it all isn't going to change that. Besides, I really don't want her knowing all the dirty secrets of the kids at school. I won't be a rat. I'm sure that's what everyone expects me to do, but I won't. "Just let me sleep, okay?"

She stands then, grabs the peas and walks away. I can hear her walk into the kitchen and open the freezer. She comes back and sets a new bag of frozen veggies, carrots, on the pillow. "Use this." And then she is gone.

I take the carrots and carefully lay the bag on my right eye and nose and eventually fall back asleep.

I spend the rest of Saturday in bed or in front of the TV, watching rerun after rerun of "Law and Order" with Dad, who never asks me anything. For dinner we have steamed carrots and peas with macaroni and cheese. My mom and dad, thankfully, have no comments about dinner or my eye, so it is a quiet evening. I go to bed early, not caring to go out on the roofs.

Sunday morning Dad actually brings me a cup of coffee and sets it down by my bed as I watch him quietly. "Your mom went to another Buddhist meeting at the Hopkins'." He leaves the room, closing the door behind him.

I decide I have had enough of pouting about my pathetic life, so I put in My Bloody Valentine, a name which is suddenly funny, and start my morning ritual, which ends in a mind orgy of long bare legs, shaking breasts, flaming red hair, and Sarah's pointy tits.

My mom is back to her talkative self after she comes back from Lara's. I am just a little irritated that she didn't invite me, even though there is no way I ever would have gone.

"Oh, Sean, you should have been there! I did the whole book with them. It was slow but they were all so patient. Lara even showed me the words, pointing to them as we went so I could follow." Now she is just rubbing it in. To sit next to Lara with her finger on the book that I hold...

"And they gave me my own beads and a book too." She pulls them out a small bag and sets them gently on the table. Then she goes back into the bag. "And these beads are for you. Lara wanted me to tell you that she bought them in Japan. Japan! Can you believe it? They go once a year."

I look at the beads my mom holds out for me. They are almost white, but woody looking, with four small green beads and two large green beads on either side. They are really, really nice. Nice? No, they are amazing. And Lara bought them for me! Oh, God, what an idiot I am. She bought the beads before she knew me. She probably bought them for Todd, and just gave them to me out of some weird sense of pity and guilt.

"Well," my mom prods. "Aren't they beautiful? They are bamboo."

Bamboo. "Yeah, they're nice." I hand them back to her, not wanting to think any more about Lara.

"We learned about Karma today, Sean." She leans over to me and gently brushes the hair out of my eyes. She looks like she is about to kiss me, so I turn away. "Did you know everything that happens to us has a cause? And an effect? So getting punched at some party was a result of past causes that you made!"

This declaration of karma as my mom's new truth is annoying. "Maybe I don't buy that, Mom."

"I guess it doesn't matter if you buy it or not, Sean."

I can't believe how easily she believes all the crap people shovel at her. I would never believe anything that easily! "Well, maybe I am with Lucinda and I believe in

God." I'm yelling now. "And some kind of grand plan that includes me getting beat in the face by the school bigshit and then hit on by the Todd wannabe!"

"So it was Todd," my mom says thoughtfully.

"What? Who hit on you?" Dad asks, obviously more concerned with me getting hit on by a guy. This is so out of his realm. Poor guy.

"Just forget it, okay?" and I go back to my room, slam the door, and sit on the floor with my CDs. That's where I stay all day. At one point, I hear my parents leaving, and I wonder what they do when they leave. Like, what do you do in a town like this on a Sunday afternoon?

That night for dinner things actually start looking up when my mom tells me I can go to Minneapolis. Dad says, "Yes, maybe that is what you need. But you can't take our car, so we have decided to buy you your own, uhm, vehicle."

"What?" I sit in disbelief. "You are letting me drive by myself to Minneapolis *and* you are going to buy me a car?"

"Well, not a car, a truck. I need something that can transport my tools, and it seems like the appropriate kind of ride around here."

"Okay, when do we get to go truck shopping?" I ask, my head still reeling at everything they just told me. Maybe I should get beat up more often. The whole sympathy factor is really working for me!

"Tomorrow, after school I will take you to Prairieville. There's a used car place there, and then I'll have to come back and finish up at the school later."

"Okay." Okay. This all seems too easy.

Even though I'm not looking forward to showing up to school with a black eye or seeing Luke, there is another part of me that is just excited that I get to go back home and see my friends in my own car, well, truck. Whatever, it is definitely more good news than bad, and that is the only thing that gets me to walk through those big metal doors and up the four flights of stairs toward my locker.

When I get to the fourth floor, though, all eyes are on me. Clearly, news of the party has traveled throughout the entire junior and senior students, and no one tries to hide their stares and smirks. I imagine some even point and laugh. I just keep reminding myself that I only have five more days, and then I will be back in Minneapolis. I have already decided I will surprise Trenton. It's gonna be awesome to see his face.

"Faggot." I hear it, followed by some giggles. And when I look back, I don't recognize anyone in the group.

I keep walking, feeling heavier.

"How are you doing?" Lindsey comes up behind me with Dan trailing behind her. When I look at her, there is genuine concern in her eyes, and I smile a little.

"Oh, man," she laughs. "You should really avoid that smiling thing. It looks painful."

"It is." I fight back tears as my face settles back into a less painful grimace.

Dan pats my shoulder tentatively, "I'm sorry we brought you to that party. I didn't know..."

Dan looks away, and I feel myself redden. Even he thinks I am gay now. And that Luke is my secret lover? Christ, what's next? But he isn't being mean about it. In fact, he touched me. I'm sure that took guts.

"I'm not, you know, gay," I say quietly, stopping in front of my locker

"We know," says Lindsey. "We would never think that about you."

Feeling a little defensive, thinking about Trenton, I say, "Well, I don't think it is a bad thing. It's just not who I am, you know?"

"Okay," says Dan awkwardly. "We should get going, Lindsey."

"Bye," Lindsey says and walks away with Dan. Yeah. Bye. No "see you later"—just bye.

So now I will spend the rest of the school year defending myself against being gay? And what about Luke? Jesus, Luke. I am thankful that I don't see him today. He must have stayed home. I don't see Todd either, though. I did, however, see Lara. She comes into English at the last minute wearing jeans and a t-shirt. She turns a little, looks at my face, and both winces and smiles a little. It sends my heart pounding, and I have a hard time taking my good eye off her the whole hour.

After class, she walks out quickly, not looking back at me again.

For lunch, I go out to my spot on the auditorium stairs, but I stop quickly, realizing I'm not alone; she is sitting on top of the big cement pillar. I start to turn and walk away thinking she might not want to see me.

"Wait," Lara says. "Come sit next to me." She pats the cement block.

She suddenly looks shy. I just stand there staring at her, wondering if I heard her right.

"Unless you don't want to. That's fine." The way she pulls her arms around her knees and pulls them into her chest breaks my heart. It is so vulnerable.

"No, I don't..." I am finally able to move, but not speak. I just shut my mouth and will my legs to move toward her. I sit next to her, too cautiously, and lean back against the cool concrete right beside her. I stretch my legs out, trying to get comfortable. I have a totally irrational image of her crawling into my lap and laying her head down on my chest, of smelling her hair. She stretches out her legs next to mine and I notice that she is wearing skinny jeans too, but that her ballet flats only reach my calves. "So what's up?" I ask, trying to be casual.

She looks at me then, I can feel it, and I turn toward her. Our heads are only a foot apart. When I look into her eyes, I find it impossible to look away—those dark eyes are so disconcerting. Then her hand moves up to my face. She gently touches the stud above my good eye. Her touch is so light, but it stings in a very good way, and I flinch a little.

"Does it hurt?" she asks pulling her hand away. Man, why did I move?

"No, not at all." I want to grab her hand and put it back on my face, but I can't move. I am still confused by the intensity of her eyes on my face. I just stare dumbly at her.

And then she does the most incredible thing! She reaches up again and touches my bangs, lifting them a little and letting them fall again, but she doesn't bring her hand down.

Her hand, wavering there, and her eyes staring into mine, make me think this must be the moment, the perfect set-up for a first kiss. I stare at her and then lean in. I can see in her eyes many emotions as I get closer and closer and I sense her hesitance but also her desire, so I reach up behind her neck and twist my fingers through her soft hair and put my lips on hers. She hesitates, but I don't back away, and then she kisses me back, slowly parting her lips, and then pushing forward more as my lips begin to part. I am lost in the movement of our lips together, sucking in her sweet breath like it is the only air I need.

But then almost as soon as it begins, it is gone. She pulls away and looks down. Is she angry? She looks angry. But why angry, I mean, what did she expect would happen?

What did I do besides what she wanted me to do?

When she looks back there are tears in her eyes, and my heart drops. Jesus, the absolute last thing I wanted to do to her was make her cry. What do I do now?

I think she sees my agony, for she wipes her eyes quickly before her tears fall, and she says, "I'm sorry. I just didn't expect that."

"No, I'm sorry. I'm so sorry! I just, you are so beautiful, and I look in your eyes, and I can't focus. I can't think... I'm sorry." The words come out with so much urgency. I want to say more, but I can't tell where I stand with her. I feel like I am dangling from a thin string about to snap. I look out then from our perch, out over the town I hate. I want the moment to end. Actually, I just want to rewind a bit. I could have just sat there and let her touch my face if that was what she wanted to do. Why did I have to ruin it?

"No, no, don't apologize," she says, smiling a little. "I didn't know you," she looks down again, "felt that way."

"You didn't?" I stare at her. What does she think I have been thinking about when I stare at her?

"Well," and now she looks embarrassed, and I feel bad again. "I actually didn't think you liked..." and she can't finish her sentence, so I look away, trying to be patient as she struggles for the words.

And then in a whisper she says, "Girls. I didn't think you liked girls."

It feels like she punched me in the gut, and I stand up fast, kind of swaying. How can I have been so stupid? Of course she thinks I am gay. I mean every other person in this town thinks I am gay, so why wouldn't she. She grew up here too. Buddhist or not, she is just as ignorant as everyone else. Her and big head Todd belong together. She is just nice to me because she has some morbid curiosity about the freak show. If she lived in "the cities"

95

she would have been a fag hag.

She groans and reaches out and touches my back, but I walk away. I can't even look at her. It is much easier to be angry and walk away, so that is what I will myself to do—walk down the auditorium steps. I keep walking down the winding steps that lead to the sidewalk.

"Sean?" She calls lamely. I won't look back. I walk home quickly. I don't notice anything but the pain in my gut.

Slamming the door to my room, I lie down in my bed, hitting the mattress hard, and start screaming at the ceiling the same way Trenton and I used to scream under the railroad track bridge when the train would roar over us. I only stop when I remember I live over a library.

Chapter 11: Suck

I am still lying in bed when I hear my mom stomping up the stairs. "See-See?"

"Yeah?" I mumble.

"Where did you go? You left early. Does it hurt?" she asks while walking to me and reaching down like she is about to touch my eye.

I suck in a breath hoping she doesn't touch it and that stops her. She just hovers over me and frowns. "Your dad," she starts. "I don't know. Maybe this isn't such a good idea."

"What, Mom?"

"Well, your dad is looking for you. He wants to go look at trucks." She makes a face. I'm not sure why.

"Okay," I pull myself up off my bed, partly because I don't want to talk to her about skipping school, but also because suddenly I am clear about everything. I am getting a new truck. I am going home, to Minneapolis. Screw Lara and Luke and Todd and all their issues. I don't even need friends here. I already have friends, and maybe even a girlfriend if Sarah still wants me. This is a sentence, and I just have to live through it. I don't need the drama. Well, not the real kind anyway.

Dad and I drive together to Prairieville. Thankfully, in silence.

The used car lot is just a field on the side of town with a bunch of old, rusted beaters parked. There are minivans and some big old cars and one truck. It is blue with a white watery looking stripe, huge, rusting a little around the tires, and kind of beautiful. I laugh when Dad and I sit in it to test drive, imagining what my friends will think. I could probably pile ten kids in the back cab area. Back cab! I am already starting to think like a trucker.

It isn't exactly easy to drive the thing. I can't see the road as well as I can in my parent's car, and it seems to not like turning, so I have to slow way down. Dad is super patient with my driving, but he talks on and on about using the gears in "weather," whatever that means, and changing the oil.

"I want to learn to do all that, Dad," I say as we pull onto Main Street. Suddenly, I want to take care of the truck all myself. At least it will give me something to do in this hideous town.

"Really?" He says, looking me over carefully. "Are you okay? Are you Sean, or some other boy who is trying to take the place of my son?"

He thinks he is so funny! I just stare blankly at him.

"Okay, clearly you are my son. You really want to learn how to change the oil?" He looks ecstatic. I feel a strange pull. It is the first time he has looked at me this way. It's not like Dad isn't proud of me. He is, but he never really gets what I do, what I'm good at. And what the hell am I good at? I used to be a good actor and a good dancer, but that feels like a lifetime ago. Maybe I need to broaden what I'm good at. Maybe if I walk around with oil on my hands people won't think I'm gay.

"I'm sure. I want to learn everything. I want to change the engine and stuff too."

He laughs. "Okay, so don't let me ever hear you say that again." He is smiling when I turn to look at him. He goes on. "You don't change the engine, Sean, at least, we better not have to, but don't worry, I'll teach you everything you need to know to take care of this beast."

I pull the truck up beside our car in front of the library, and for something so big and hideous, it fits in on this main street quite well. We sit quietly for a couple minutes.

"Sean, are you okay? Is this okay?"

"Yeah, Dad. The truck is great." I know what he is asking, and I am not interested in talking about anything, so I smile at him, wincing a little at the pain between my eyes and start getting out of the truck.

He sighs and says, "Lessons start tomorrow. Have the truck outside the ag shop doors around 4:30. We can pull it in and check the oil."

Dad is very thorough in teaching me about my truck. Every day after school for that whole week we do something new—I'm not a complete lost cause either. It is, actually, the only time I really feel comfortable. School is generally quite bad. Lara avoids me, Todd and Luke do too. Luke and Todd seem all buddy-buddy again, which is totally mystifying, but whatever, I can't be bothered. Dan, Jasper, Michelle, and Lindsey are nice still, but I feel like a fifth wheel when I am with them.

When Mrs. Halestrom announces that there will be winter play try-outs on Friday for Dracula, I feel the first peak of hope. Who cares that I found the book tedious on the second read, that I played Dracula before; it is at least the stage, and surely I won't have a hard time getting a lead part. I am thinking maybe Dracula again or Helsinki. Or maybe I can try out for Madame Mina. Sadly, I don't think anyone would be surprised if I did.

Considering this, I walk into the bathroom. Usually, when I go, I choose a stall, but no one is there, so I take one of the urinals. Just as I start, of course, someone walks in, and the footsteps come right up beside me. He could have chosen two or three down, but he is right there. I try not to look over, but I can feel him staring at me, so I glance, annoyed, over at him, noticing it is a football player but not one that I know by name.

"Don't look at me, faggot."

I'm still not done, but as soon as I am able to stop, I button up and walk out.

"Football season does end, you know. You are dead meat for fucking with Luke and Todd. Watch your back."

My heart is slamming in my chest. He is still pissing, and I want to run at him, run him into his own piss, but instead I just walk out.

Friday finally comes, nearly ending the hideous week. Try-outs are in the gym during lunch hour, so I shuffle there feeling oddly nervous. I can't believe my eyes when I walk into the auditorium, and half the school is there! Are all these people trying out? I take a seat in the back and watch for a while, trying to get a handle on it.

Mrs. Halestrom moves to the center of the basketball court, which has been transformed with the heavy curtains into an actual stage, and says in her best stage voice, "Ladies and gentlemen, this is not a show. These are try-outs, and unless you seriously plan to be a part of this play and try out, I suggest you all scoot on to your lunch or class."

I notice most of the football team, including psycho pisser, is down in front complaining at this point, and Luke stands up and says, "We have every right to be here. We want to support Todd."

Mrs. Halestrom smiles, but I can tell she is irritated. What the hell is up with Luke? All of a sudden he is the spokesman for the football team? Talk about over compensating! "Please," Mrs. Halestrom interrupts the grumbling. "You are all very noble in your desire to support your teammate, but if Todd cannot do this without all of your support, then he should reconsider trying out at this time."

Ouch, that was a nice jab at Todd. Good!

"Those of you who are trying out for Dracula, please move to the front of the auditorium. The rest of you... clear out!"

As most of the other students "clear out," the football players walk behind me out the door. I am pushed forward hard in my chair, and when I look back, there are four guys, two are psycho pisser and Luke, laughing at me. I feel a stab of sadness that Luke is including himself in the Sean hater group, but what the fuck? What did I do? They keep walking out the door, and I slowly walk up to the front. Michelle and Jasper are there. Does he let her do anything by herself? Lara's there, and so is Todd. Jen is there too and a bunch of other people I haven't met yet.

Mrs. Halestrom seems pleased with herself. "This is a cold reading of the play Dracula. You come up one at a time and let me know what part you are thinking to play, and I will give you a couple parts to read."

"Okay, I'm ready," yells Todd, jumping to his feet.

"Todd? You want to start? Well, come on up."

Todd and Mrs. Halestrom talk a little when he gets up onto the stage, she hands him the script, and he jumps into the middle of the stage. He reads the Dracula part, of course, lathering on a fake accent that sounds completely unreal.

"Tame down the accent, Todd," Mrs. Halestrom instructs, "but keep going. You are doing well."

Todd calms down and starts to sound pretty good. I am mainly just impressed that he knows how to read.

A couple other people go up next, one reading Dracula and one reading Mina. Why does everyone think they can be the star?

When Lara goes up, I watch enraptured. She reads Lucy, and I can't imagine a better Lucy myself. And despite our earlier humiliating kiss, as she declares her love for Jonathan, I make up my mind as to who I will try out for. I will make her squirm. She kissed me back, damn it!

I don't fake an accent when I read Jonathan's part. I play it cool, a little boring and clueless, as I imagine Jonathan to be. I can tell no one is particularly awed with my rendition, but Mrs. Halestrom looks impressed, and she is all that counts.

After a few more, Michelle stands up. As she passes my chair, she looks at me and winks. Winks! Then she slowly walks up the stairs.

By the end of her part of the reading, she is kneeling at the feet of Mrs. Halestrom, pleading and clutching the script with one hand and Halestrom's knee with the other. "You can have no idea of what an evil man he is or the terrible things he does. I could not... dare not... try to leave on my own. He would find me again, I know. But, with you to help me, I would have a chance. Oh, you must help me. You must! You're my only hope. You must!"

Mrs. Halestrom, uncomfortable with the physical contact, but clearly entertained by Michelle's performance, says stiffly, "I'll help you, I promise. Please don't distress yourself."

Michelle rises, and I can see Mrs. Halestrom holding her breath. I can't help but giggle a little, and a couple people look at me. Michelle stands and says in her best psychotic voice, "Thank you," and then she dives in to bite the neck of our English teacher, who steps back quickly from the embrace and says, "Very good, Michelle. Very... umm... believable."

Michelle then turns to the audience, blushing wildly, and runs down the steps. As she sits down, I catch her eye and raise an eyebrow. She was great!

After school, my mom and dad are standing outside my truck leaning into the window reciting lists of things. Dad's list is mostly about the truck and driving. Mom's list is about calling and driving and not drinking and saying hello to all my friends and giving Trenton a hug, and finally after all that, she slips me fifty dollars. I tell them I have to go.

"It's a long way to the cities," I say putting on my best hick voice.

Dad lightly hits the back of my head and laughs. "Come on, Cheryl, let the kid go."

I smile as I turn off Main Street onto Highway 71, pass all the old lady name towns, and stop at Mickey D's to celebrate my freedom by chowing down on large fries and a Coke.

I was only away for like a month, but when the traffic starts getting thicker I am actually a little nervous about driving. I do start getting some good radio stations in though, so that helps with the nerves a bit. The college radio station is music to my ears, and they are playing Lorde; it doesn't even matter that two months ago I was cursing them for playing the same five songs over and over again. It is so good to hear something other than bad pop, classic rock, or country that I actually sing along.

I head to Trenton's house first. I find him by walking through the front door, not knocking, shaking my head that they still never lock their door. He is primping in the bathroom. I know before I look because he's singing and the door is open. I peek around the corner and scare the shit out of him. "Jesus, See! Could you at least knock, call, I don't know, let me know in some communicative way to expect you?"

"Hot date?" I smile, walking by him to sit on the toilet.

"Hot party! You've got to come, but no way in hell am I letting you wear that! What the hell are you thinking letting the hicks influence you? Is that a tee flannel layer?"

"I am at your disposal," I say lowering both arms, palms up.

Two hours later I am wearing silver and black striped dress slacks and a silver lamé, button-up shirt, and my eyes are lined expertly by Trenton, who can use liquid liner like no other. The bruises, now slight, are covered by Maybelline, and my hair is actually styled, even trimmed by Trenton, who wanted to "accentuate the angle of my long bangs.".". I like what I see when I look in the mirror, but I say, "I didn't turn gay in Eagle Peak, you know."

Trenton ignores my comment, slaps my ass, and heads out the door. I follow him, completely excited to see his look when he sees "The Beast," which I have affectionately named my truck. He doesn't disappoint. Opening the front door, he stops dead in his tracks, and slowly turns around, mouth frozen in a grimace, masking shock. I am smiling gleefully, so he bites back his comments, knowing I have already prepared comebacks.

Despite the lack of comments about The Beast, he spends most of the beginning of the party giving tours of my truck to the partygoers. I am humored by this, and allow him to keep the keys to do as he will.

I am happier than I have been in weeks. People treat me like I never left. In fact, no one asks me anything. Later, when Trenton walks in beside Sarah, I am dancing in the living room. I know the outfit looks great with seventies moves, so I shuffle over to her and pull her into a wide turn arms crossed and straight, and she laughs and flings back her head. Trenton is watching us, and I can't tell what he is thinking, but he is definitely thinking.

Later, Sarah and I are alone in one of the upstairs bedrooms.

"You've been gone. Got a girlfriend yet?"

"No. It's pretty much sucked."

"So you wanted a girlfriend?"

"No. It's just sucked, you know. Lame. Nothing to do," I say and then smile, "but climb the roofs." I wonder how my little hideout is doing? Why am I thinking about Eagle Peak? I am here, with Sarah. This is what I want. So I focus hard. "Let's not talk about it. Can we just fuck?"

"What? What the hell did you just say to me?"

Dammit! Truth be gone. Why don't I filter? "I just, I missed you," *and I have been masturbating to you for the last month every morning.* I am smart enough to leave that out.

"Okay."

"Okay what?"

"Okay. Let's... fuck."

"Well, that's good."

"Good?" she raises that eyebrow. I know the look. I know I should care that she raised the eyebrow, but I don't, so I kiss her. She kisses me back, and all I can do is think about what my mouth should be doing. Like her tongue is there, so I think, I should touch her tongue to mine. And then she kind of moans, so I try to say something. Something sexy, but then I bite my tongue a little bit and it hurts, but I don't close my mouth. I just open it and leave it like that. And I can feel her working it, but I can't think what to do. My hands are at my sides, and why the hell is that? This is nothing like what happens in my morning ritual.

She is the one to stop. "What is wrong with you? Once upon a time you knew how to kiss. Are you sure you don't have a girlfriend?"

"I just hate it there. All those kids just staring at me.

I'm a freak. That is all I am. They all think I'm gay. Even Lara."

"Lara. So she has a name?"

"Yeah, even Lara. Luke too. He's gay but doesn't want to admit it, unless he is drunk and hitting on me. Then he'll say it. Well, not say it, but he tried to kiss me."

"Well, I haven't been just sitting around pining after you, you know," she says.

"And then there's the play. I'm sure I'll get the part of Jonathan. Todd will get Dracula. He thinks he's so hot, and he's the one who did this to my eye," I say pointing to my black eyes now covered in Maybelline beige matte concealer. "And then my mom is suddenly Buddhist and goes to these meetings every weekend at Lara's house."

"Lara again."

"It's just all screwed up, you know? I don't want to get out of bed."

"Well, maybe you should just fuck Lara then!"

I hear what she says and it hurts, like she shouldn't be talking about Lara that way. Then I see what a complete ass I've been. It's okay for me to ask Sarah to fuck, but not to ask Lara that way. What does that mean?

Sarah is leaving the room, and I know she's pissed. Really pissed, and I can't bring myself to care. I lay back on the bed, not knowing whose bed it is, and close my eyes.

Trenton wakes me up. He's mad too and really really screechy. It hurts my ears.

"You can't just come here and hurt Sarah, Sean. I don't care if we were once best friends. Sarah is here and she is a good friend, and I don't want you breaking her heart so that I am left to pick up the pieces."

"What do you mean, 'she's here?' What, you think I had a choice in moving?" I can't believe how insensitive everyone is being. No one even asked me how I was or what is going on.

"No, but it doesn't change the fact, does it?" Trenton is staring down at me. He looks disgusted.

"I don't know why I came here. I'm just gonna drive home," I say and get up to leave.

"You can't just drive home at one in the morning! You'll fall asleep at the wheel and die, and now wouldn't that fuck Sarah up!"

"Sarah? Is that all you can think about?" I am yelling now, and Trenton is cringing. I know he doesn't like to be yelled at, but I can't help myself. "What about me? What about all the hell I am going through? And now my old friends aren't even my friends."

It isn't until Trenton hugs me that I realize that I'm crying, and then it's over. I become a sobbing mess. "Okay," he says. "Let's go to my place. You can crash there and we can talk."

"Yeah," I say into Trenton's wet neck.

We go to Angry Catfish Coffee in the morning, and even the cute, most probably not gay, baristas can't shake Trenton out of his angry silent punishment of my lapse.

We sit at the high table that overlooks the street. It's nice to see people dressed fashionably, or not, with different styles. I look at Trenton brooding over his mocha, his skin dark and shiny, his hair longer and fluffier than usual, wearing a plain white t-shirt and a V-neck orange vest over it, snug over royal blue skinny jeans. He can make the dorkiest clothes look urban chic, and very, very gay. I do love him, but I'm too pissed to acknowledge his self-inflicted prissiness. If he were a loyal friend, we'd be having a nice time right now. But he's turned into a Sarah supporter—the traitor.

We watch passersby quietly until I really can't stand it and tell him I have to go home.

"Yeah," Trenton says. "I gotta study for a chem test."

I turn to stare now, really looking at him. He looks tired, but there's no way in hell that he's going to study this afternoon.

Trenton knows my looks. "What? I study now. People change, right?"

I know he's full of shit, and that is why I end up coming home Saturday instead of Sunday.

Getting in my car to go home really sucks. I consider going out to eat or something, but I am so tired. I just get gas, one of those 5-hour energy drinks, and drive. Two hours and twenty-four minutes and three turns later, I arrive in front of the library. I look up and am happy to see lights on. I run around back, up the stairs and into the apartment, and I immediately regret not calling. I can tell by the thumping on the floor, the shuffling and zipping, that I interrupted my parents. Thank God they weren't doing it on the living room couch or something! Still, the sexual trauma I have experienced this weekend is getting to me. Before they can trip out of their room and question me, I say, "It's me, I'm early—going to bed!" And I go to my room, closing the door tightly.

Chapter 12: Blanket of Snow

I wake up and my room is bright, too bright. I must have slept until noon. I look over at the clock, and it says 8:00 a.m., but I don't believe it. Shuffling to the window, eyes squinting, I see it. Across the roofs, on top of the store signs, is a blanket of white snow. And then there's the ridiculousness, also known as Main Street. Four lone tracks of tires and a plow driving down the street, pushing the snow, not to the side but to the middle, leaving a trail of snow, kind of like a really lame Mohawk, right down the middle of the road. "Idiots," I mumble to myself and turn to put on some music loud and lay back down.

My mom peeks in after some time of blissful noise. "Are you coming?"

"Where?" When a flat out no is what I really want to say.

"To Gerald and Janine's for the meeting." She walks in carrying a cup of coffee.

"Snowstorm," I mumble.

"Whatever, Sean. That is like one inch of snow, hardly enough to matter. It'll probably melt while we are there."

"No, Mom, I don't want to go, okay?"

She sits on my bed, sets the coffee on the floor, and puts her hand on my forehead.

"I'm not sick," I say, turning away.

She grabs my chin then, turns my head to her and

stares into my eyes. I know the look so well—it is the one to break me, and I try to look away again.

"Don't turn away. I feel like I haven't looked at you in a long time. Let me look. I'm your mother."

And I look up at her. Her eyes just keep looking into my eyes, and I feel like she can see inside me because her eyes change from laughing to really, really sad. And that makes me sad, and I can't stop tears from popping out. She just keeps looking at me, so I stare back and let the tears fall down my cheek, and then she says, "Oh, See-See. Your dad and I didn't really think this through, did we? This is hard for you."

Um, understatement? I can't say anything because I'm worried I'll start sobbing and blubbering.

"Tell me the truth. Do you want to move back?"

What? Move back? She's asking me that now? Like her and Dad would leave their jobs? "We would, you know. We would for you if you really needed it."

I think about Trenton and Sarah and know they don't want me back. "No, I don't think so."

She lets go and gets up to leave. "Drink the coffee," she says. "Let's go chant. I think it will help."

We walk into Lara's house. It is a little smoky with incense, and I hear Gerald chanting as Janine is waving us up the stairs.

As we are walking through the kitchen, Janine leans into me and says, "Lara's not here. She is at a friend's house."

I nod and follow her.

My mom hands me my bamboo beads, and I put them on. They feel good, and the chanting is soothing. I really like the Daimoku part, where we just chant the same thing over and over. The repetition is easier than trying to read along in the book.

I am totally relaxed by the time the chanting ends. Gerald turns around. "So today we will discuss the Buddhist teaching 'winter always turns into spring.' I thought that would be appropriate given the weather we are having."

I look at my mom, and she is nodding and smiling, like she knows. Janine does too, and Gerald looks like he's unlocking the secret to the fucking universe. I start laughing a little.

Gerald turns to me. "Sean, what do you think that means?" His legs are folded under him and he is leaning forward a little.

"Sounds pretty obvious to me," I say, ignoring my mom's glare. I am in no mood to be friendly.

Gerald smiles. "Yes, there is an obvious aspect to it, but what do you think the not-so-obvious is?"

I roll my eyes. Like he is the only one in this room who can unravel a metaphor. "Well, that all our troubles will turn out fine, I guess."

"Not exactly," says Gerald. "I think it means that if we keep chanting throughout our troubles, our difficulties will turn into a rebirth of sorts—we will grow from them. You can't have spring without winter—if the weather is nice and warm all the time, there would be no need to call it anything."

"So LA doesn't have spring?" I ask, smirking.

Gerald laughs. "Good question! If they do, I bet they don't appreciate it as much as we do. It just seems the colder the winter is, the nicer the spring is."

"Well, sounds like I am in for a hot summer." I'm half-sarcastic and half-serious.

"Sometimes you just have to wait through the winter," he says quietly and then turns to ring the bell for Sansho, where we chant Nam-myoho-renge-kyo three times slowly.

Then we leave and go home. And the little snow that we had is melting, as predicted by my sage-like mother.

I walk up the hill to school Monday morning through some new snow, and half the school is out on the front lawn. Most everyone I recognize, and there is a pang of feeling at knowing everyone. Each class is under their sign. When I look under the junior sign, I recognize everyone. Dan, Lindsey, Jasper, and Michelle are all there. The football players are running around pelting each other with slushballs, and the cheerleaders are buzzing around in blue and yellow. The teachers are trying to organize everyone into teams or something. The whole scene is both trippy and horrifying.

Michelle walks up to me as I attempt to avoid the chaos and go in the side door. "You can run, but you cannot hide from..." and then she waves her arms theatrically, "homecoming!"

"Hmm... homecoming. Nope, not familiar with that."

She smirks, clearly getting my humor, and grabs my hand, pulling me to the band geeks, a.k.a. my only remaining, very tentative, friends. "By the way, you really have to check out the try-out results outside of Halestrom's classroom."

"Whatever," I say, resenting being pulled around.

She smiles at me. "Ah, Sean, I know you care."

Dan and Jasper are laughing as we walk up, but Jasper stops as soon as he sees Michelle holding my hand. Michelle seems to not notice and tightens her grip. Or maybe that means she did notice. At any rate, I am feeling a tad uncomfortable in this love triangle and pull away from Michelle,who looks a little injured as I do.

I walk into the building to where the Dracula results are posted, and there are no shocks. I am Jonathan, Lara is Mina, Todd is Dracula, and Michelle is psycho vampiress. Even Jasper has a part. Hmm, should be a really fun time! Why do I keep getting in the middle of these people?

Later in the day, after some humiliating "snow games," which are basically the teachers and the geeks getting pelted with ice balls, getting back into class is a relief. At one point, Lindsey pulls me aside to explain the latest news in my circle of friends—Jasper and Michelle broke up! Wow, big shocker there. And I have a feeling who Michelle is gauging as her next boy toy. Ugh!

The whole week is a bit of a blur. It mostly consists of the students dressing up in dumb outfits, like pajamas on pajama day. A bunch of the senior girls have to be sent home, but I hear they had vehemently argued tanks and boy shorts were what they actually wear as pajamas. Sixties day is another oddity—girls in poodle skirts and high ponytails. I spend my time most of the week avoiding all human contact since the whole school seems to have gone mad. Mrs. Halestrom gives everyone the task of memorizing their lines this week. Todd wears his vampire teeth most of the week, and it's getting so annoying. Most of the teachers tell him he has to take them off in class. It only takes me a few days to memorize all my lines.

It is Friday morning, and I am staring absently into my open locker, mystified by all the crap I have accumulated. I actually have extra shoes, notebooks, books, pens, pencils, eyeliner, a calculator, and other accouterments haphazardly shoved into corners.

I feel someone squeezing up and under my arms and look down to the red hair of Michelle. I back up and say, "Well, hello. Can I help you?"

"Oh, me? Now that you ask, yes, you can."

She is an odd duck.

"I, uhm, Jasper and I, you know. Broke up. And now I don't have anyone to take me to the dance tonight. The homecoming dance?"

"Hmm, that's too bad, but you seem to dance just fine on your own," I say.

She takes a step forward, invading my personal space again. "But that doesn't mean I want to. Please? Can you take me to the dance?"

Oh, God, she had to say please. And she looks so desperate. What could be the harm in that? "Okay. What time?"

"Oh, thanks," she says going in for a hug. I manage to not step back, and the force of her hug hurts a little where she squeezes. "Come about 8:00 p.m. to my place. I should be done with marching band stuff for the game tonight, and I'll be ready to go. Here," she says pulling out a sheet of paper from her baggy jeans. "Here are directions."

"Directions?" I say. Does the madness end? I look down, and her handwriting and road lines are meticulously drawn—a yellow highlighter marking a clear path from the library to her house in timbuck fuck.

"See you later, Sean. It's a dance, so dress festive!" And then she is off, skipping down the hall, her red hair bouncing down her back. I turn back to my open locker, shaking my head.

Chapter 13: Homecoming

It feels right to drive up to Michelle's house in my truck, kind of farmy, but the smells that assault me when I get out of the truck make me want to carry Febreeze and spray it everywhere—the smell of poop and corn are a really bad combination. I walk slowly to the house, trying to breathe through my mouth, wondering what the hell I am doing going on a date with Michelle. But then I remember her flute playing and the feel of her little waist under her sweatshirt when we danced. I wonder what variety of sweats she will wear tonight.

I start to feel weird about my attire. I didn't bother to tone it down tonight—green glass earrings, my "Dead Kennedys" t-shirt under a black polyester suit jacket and slacks and my shiny patent leather shoes. I should feel dapper, but walking up to this farmhouse, I don't.

Before I get to the door, it swings open and I am being shot at by the standard finger gun of her little brother. I clutch my chest and lean back, but I don't fall down because I'm worried there might be cow shit or something on the ground, so I stumble a little—obviously satisfactory for him, because he yelps a victory cry and disappears into the house. I walk the rest of the way and stop when what I presume to be her father shows up in the door. He fills the door, really. He's one of those guys with the massive neck and belly, who looks like he sits in a lazy boy and drinks beer.

"Sean?" he says in a nice deep voice, and I am surprised that he says it right.

"That's me," I say extending a hand.

He shakes it firmly and waves me in. I manage to get around his belly without rubbing up against him and come face to face with Lucinda, the red haired librarian, and am speechless. For one irrational moment I wonder what the hell the librarian is doing here. Then she says, "Hi, Sean. Do you remember me? I am Lucinda, Michelle's mom." She is smiling in that aggressively expectant way she did in the library, and I am unsure again of what reaction will come out of my mouth.

"Uh-huh," I say lamely. I look around, pretending to care about the photos on the wall as they watch me.

"So how is school going?" she asks.

I don't really feel like talking at the moment. I am trying to process the fact that this nosy librarian is Michelle's mom!

It is the boy who saves me. He comes shooting down the stairs like a bullet, squealing as Michelle flies down after him screaming, "Give it back, you twerp!"

I am caught between laughter and shock at the ridiculousness of the scene, but stop any reaction when her dad catches the boy and swings him up into his arms and she stops beside me panting, hand outstretched, waiting. The kid drops what seems to be a necklace in her open hand. "Brat!" she says.

"Michelle!" Lucinda says loudly. "Give me that necklace. Oh, look at you, aren't you pretty," her mom says, and then I see she is tearing up.

Michelle looks at me and rolls her eyes but gives the necklace to her mom, who shakes as she tries to open it. Michelle turns her back to us, and I can tell her mom is struggling with the clasp, her father looking on helplessly. I wonder briefly why she is trembling, and I can tell she is getting frustrated.

"Let me," I say, taking the necklace from her trembling hands.

She frowns and I turn to Michelle's bare neck. I am close enough now to smell the hair spray in her hair, which is a mass of red curls.

"Thanks," Michelle says, turning shyly and winking. I notice then that her eyes, a really stunning green color, are lined in black. I let my eyes drop down her body to notice the smallness and blackness of her outfit—a tight, skin tight actually, dress and fishnet tights, and I feel the urge to turn because I am suddenly getting a boner to be put on display to her librarian mom, massive dad, and bratty brother.

Thankfully, she grabs my hand and swings me around, and we are heading out the door.

"Bye," she yells. "I'll be home by one."

"One? Doesn't the dance end at like eleven?"

She pats my hand then, patronizing. "I'm sure we can figure something out."

I look down at her, a little afraid, and the fact that the girl beside me in her fishnet tights and ultra white skin is practically skipping doesn't help ease my mind.

I open the door to my truck for her, and she slinks around me and blushes at the same time.

"No flute tonight?"

"Nah, Katy Perry and Lady Antebellum here we come!" she says giving me a thumbs up that looks kind of dorky. She's trying to be dorky, of course, but she doesn't pull it off in a funny way. Sarah could do funny dorky. Michelle can't. It just looks desperate.

I close the door and walk around the front, and I try to convince myself not to be an ass to her. She's so sweet, yet she's not. What do I know about her? The first time I met her she was writhing on the library floor having just died at the hands of her brother, and the second time she was gyrating on top of the gravel mountain, totally uninhibited as she wailed out The Pixies with her flute. Now she plays the picture of subdued shyness. Really? Shy? In fishnets? They remind me of Sarah's Halloween costume last year—a pirate with fishnet stockings and metallic little fish stuck on her legs, trapped in the netting.

With that, I get into the truck and slam the door hard.

"Thanks for doing this," Michelle says, smiling at me. She looks pretty when she smiles like that. Then we drive quietly to the school, not listening to any music since all The Beast can get is country stations.

We walk into the gym and stand in the doorway, giving a minute for our eyes to adjust. Thank God for streamers—blue and gold all over the place! How else could this lame school create a festive environment? It looks haphazard, and with the disco light, I can feel an epileptic fit coming on. True to her prediction, Lady Antebellum, who I sadly recognize, is talking about running to someone. Kids are standing in the middle of the gym, some of them jumping, some of them swaying, but none of it could be considered dancing.

Jen comes sashaying up to us. "Hey, y'all." She's got the worst southern drawl that I've ever heard, but she is clueless. "Wow, guys. You really dressed up for this." Jen is wearing skin-tight jeans and a tank top, as if she just threw it on in a last minute attempt to get to this dance.

Michelle smiles. "Don't worry, Jen, you can wear anything and pull it off."

I turn quickly to see Michelle staring at Jen, still smiling that sweet clueless smile. That was an incredibly appropriate slam, and Jen walks off without another comment.

Michelle giggles a little as she sees the shock in my face and grabs my hand. She pulls me to the DJ. I hear her yell, "Do you have any Butthole Surfers?" Yeah, as if... classic punk doesn't seem the speed of Eagle Peak.

"Who?" the guy says. "What do they sing?"

"Um... well, Pepper?" Again, I am shocked. This girl is brilliant! Of course they'd have that song.

"Yeah, we have that."

"You put in Pepper and this young man and I will cut a rug!" She does the thumbs up again and this time she looks kind of cute.

And as we walk through the standers, Pepper begins with a simple shaky beat and then the telltale white guy rap. Michelle, who I was pretty sure had no sense of rhythm, starts to waltz, dragging me along in the process. And it works, the waltz. We swing through the crowds of awkward looking kids who have no idea what to do with the Butthole Surfers. We spin by Lara, who is standing and watching. I wonder briefly why she doesn't dance in public, but don't think about it too long because I am starting to have real fun with Michelle. The four minutes of the song pass so quickly, I am a little unhappy when it winds down. Maybe there will be another polka beat, but I'm not hopeful.

As the song eases into the Dixie Chicks, Michelle spins out of my arms, and I feel a little pull. She starts to jump and pump her arms spastically. She doesn't look exactly good doing it, but then I see her face, and see something that I haven't felt in some time now—joy. She is totally lost in the music, and I don't think she cares what anyone thinks of her. I am drawn in, and I start to mimic the spasms. She laughs at my "attempts." I start feeling comfortable enough to pull out the moves I usually save for cooler scenes. I am hustling, popping, and totally dripping in sweat by the end of the dance. Nope, polyester doesn't breathe.

Later, we are in my loft space above the senior citizen's center. "Your parents are so cool," Michelle says, taking a swig of the beer Dad let us bring out with us. "They didn't stop us from going out on the roofs and they gave us beer!"

"One beer. Hardly enough to do any damage." I take the beer from her hand and sip. I am so happy there is heat seeping up through the floor, but it is still a little chilly. Part of me feels protective of this space, and I wonder if it is right to bring her here.

"Well, if you stop drinking it and let me down it, you could maybe get me tipsy and take advantage of me."

"That's not really my style," I say, wishing it were. Her fish-netted legs are slung over my legs and she keeps inching closer for warmth. I hand her the bottle.

She gulps down the rest of it and belches loudly, smiling up at me. I can smell-taste the beer and what she ate last—it smells like meat. Gross. I want to gag, but she is so damn cute with her little fairy face and the big lips that work wonders on a flute. I don't turn away.

I can see in her eyes that she is considering kissing me, and I guess I'm considering it too, but then the moment passes and it just feels awkward.

"Yeah," she says, smiling.

"Yeah," I agree. But I'm not sure what I am agreeing to. "Let's just..." And then I lean in and our lips touch. I'm waiting, maybe we're both waiting, for the electricity to happen. She opens her eyes, her lips still on mine and then she crosses her eyes and starts cracking up. I laugh with her, bummed that my life couldn't be easier—perhaps she's thinking the same thing.

She surprises me then and shifts over my body to straddle me, and my hands are on each thigh, her dress hitched up to her waist. I like the feeling of skin between the strings, so I just let my hands walk up her thighs.

When she makes a sound between a squeak and a sigh, I can feel myself getting hard, and I pull her in close.

Her hands are squeezing the back of my head as her lips land on mine. The thought crosses my mind that I hope I don't taste meat when we kiss, and I am happy that all I taste is a little beer and something kind of sweet and salty—Michelle. Then I'm not thinking and I pull her even closer. She falls over me and starts moving her hips over my jeans—I can actually feel her warmth through the jeans as she rubs and rubs, and I feel like I am going to die—it feels so good and hurts so bad, like that song my mom likes. I am ready to pop out of my jeans when I feel her start to shake and moan, and I realize that she is going—she is having an orgasm, and I think this is the first time I've witnessed this, so I open my eyes and stare at her. Her red hair is flaming all around her and her cheeks are flushed, her eyes closed and her mouth open a little. I watch as the shaking rises up to her forehead—I swear I can see it twitch.

And then she opens her eyes. I expect her to be embarrassed, but she smiles a little. There is no inhibition as she peels off her dress and reaches behind her to unclasp her bra. Her breasts bounce as the bra is pulled off, and I realize then that there is a definite difference in shape. While Sarah's pointed out, Michelle's are wider and softer, and her nipples are a really light pink, almost indistinguishable, from her skin.

"Your turn," she says, and I gulp.

I don't have time to touch her breasts because she is scooting down my body, opening my shirt and licking my chest, then stomach, then... lower. I say a prayer of thanks that I am not wearing skinny jeans, and that my pants slip down with relative ease. She grabs me, and I pray that this will be my first blowjob, and I am not disappointed. She actually starts to suck on it, and within about, oh, twenty seconds, I am coming in her mouth. I hear someone cry out and realize it is me. Oh, motherfucking God, or Buddha, or whoever!

I can't move after my body stops spasming, but Michelle sits up and spits into the corner. "It's kind of gross, you know. I just can't bring myself to swallow. Did you see that movie, Something about Mary? I suppose I could use it for hair gel, but that's kind of gross too."

She is babbling, and sitting there looking kind of cold, so I grab her and pull her into my naked chest, wrapping my shirt around her. "Thanks," I say into her hair.

"Thank you!" she says back. "Umm... do you want to dance?"

No. I want to sit here and cuddle. "Okay," I say.

She stands up, her breasts bouncing as she reaches for her bra.

"Let me," I say as she reaches behind her to clasp it. This is something that I always dreamed of doing with a girl, but getting those little metal things into the other things is unbearably hard, and I have to bend down and concentrate to get it done. After the bra is clasped, I reach down and grab her dress and pull it over her head. She pushes her head and arms through and turns to look at me, kind of stuck in the dress. I kneel down and tug it for her, but I think it catches on her hair or something. "Ouch!" she cries out, but then works it free.

I grab her around the waist and pull her in to a slow dance because I am feeling completely uncoordinated by this point, but dancing is something I can do in my sleep. We sway for a bit until she says, "Well, I should be going home."

"Yeah, probably," I say. I sense that she is not thrilled with me. I can't seem to get a handle on the situation. The reality can't measure to what my dreams have been. All my life I have dreamed of this, right? Then why aren't I happier?

Getting back through the window proves equally awkward. She kind of gets stuck in the window, and, laughing, says, "Um, a little help here," her ass in my face. "Jesus, please just push so this moment will end!"

I laugh, put one hand on each butt cheek, thinking I should be turned on, but all I can really think is how mortified she must feel right now. And I give her a light shove. She slips right into the room, and I hear a thunk on the floor. Her wild red hair and face bounces up, and she gives me another thumbs up, and this time I laugh—more at her than with her. When I slink through the window, she mutters, "Show off," and stalks off.

We pull up to her house. It is so quiet in the truck, it's hard to think, so I am glad when I turn off the engine. It breaks something, and she turns to me, now shy, but she looks determined.

I grab her hand in a lame effort to wrap up the evening nicely. She looks down at my hand, up to my face, and then she leans over and kisses my cheek. "See you around," she says and starts to get out.

But I keep her hand in mine. I don't want to let go; we haven't really talked all night, and suddenly that feels important. "Do you want to talk?"

"Talk?" she asks smiling. "Um... sure. Let's go in. I think everyone is sleeping."

"Are you sure it's okay?" I ask, not really wanting to be in the same house as Lucinda, especially after her daughter and I, yeah, no, that is just way too awkward. "Is there somewhere else we can go?"

"Yeah," she says thoughtfully, "there is one place I've always wanted to check out. Always thought it was way too cheesy, but it seems right tonight."

"Gee, thanks?"

Michelle smiles. "Just drive, okay?"

I start the truck back up, turn around and head down

the driveway, thinking the whole time, what am I doing now? I almost was able to say goodbye, and then I couldn't, and now I want to again.

"I don't think you're cheesy, Sean," she finally says. "I don't know you, really. Everyone here I grew up with. Jasper and I are more friends than anything."

I snort at that. Whatever, she can keep telling herself that, but it's probably news to Jasper that she is just his "friend."

"No, really, at least from my end," she goes on. "You are this mystery. I don't know you," she says again. "I think you are sensitive, though."

"Okay, now I'm just offended." Sensitive? Not the adjective you want to hear from someone who just gave you a blowjob.

"See? You are!" she laughs. "I mean, wait, turn here, and then, yeah, see that trail there leading into the woods—that's the road you need to take."

I stop then where I am supposed to turn. "You want me to take my truck into the woods? There isn't even a trail!" The last thing I want to do is get stuck tonight.

"Oh, hell, Sean, here, just move over and let me drive."

"No!" I say, but she is already pushing one fish-netted leg over me and I am already hard, and I don't want her to know, so I quickly scoot under, out of her way. She settles behind the wheel, hikes up her skirt a little to spread her legs, and smiles over at me.

All I can do is stare.

"You have to gun it into the ditch and then ride it hard through the trail 'cause' there's brush and roots and mud that we can get hung up on. You are so not equipped to do this!" She laughs. Then she does as she warned. We fly to the left across the road, into the ditch, and then up and crash through the forest. I barely see a trail, but the narrow break in the trees is presumably the road, and then I get distracted by the branches whipping against the windows and the crazy bouncing. This can't be good for the Beast.

We stop quickly as soon as we break through the last trees. Right below I can just make out a sharp dropping hill, a gravel road, and beyond the road nothing, just blackness. And it is so quiet, even when she opens the window a little.

I wonder what to say, what to do. Michelle sits still, looking out—I can see from the lights on the dashboard how her little nose has the same sharp angle Lucinda's has, but her features aren't so blotchy as her mother's—they are finer. She is really kind of pretty. I am unfamiliar with all this. It feels like we are parking—parking in the country. I wonder if this could really be my life.

"This is weird for you, right?" she says. I just look at her. She keeps looking forward. "I mean, it's weird for you to, like, be here, in this town?"

"Yeah," I say, now looking forward. I can't read her. I don't know what she is getting at.

"It's all I know, but it's weird for me too. I never felt like I quite fit in here."

I think about that. She doesn't feel like she fits in? What must that feel like to live somewhere all your life and not feel like you fit in? "That sucks."

"Yes, yes it does," she says, turning in her seat. She shifts so one leg is crossed across the seat, which opens up her skirt even more. It is dark, but I can still see the whiteness of her legs, and I can kind of imagine the rest. "What do you want, Sean?"

She asks it so matter-of-factly that I'm not sure what she is asking. "Does it matter, Michelle?" I say loudly, using her name back. I feel kind of bitchy but what the fuck, it's how I feel.

She reaches for my hand, and I let her have it. "What do you want?"

"Truth?" I wonder out loud.

"Yeah," she says.

"Right now, I want you, but I don't really know what I'll want another day."

"Do you want to talk or make out more?" she asks.

Is she for real? "Jesus, Michelle, really? Like you are giving me a choice? What do you want?"

"Right now, I want you, but that kind of scares me because I don't know you. But it's easier to not talk, you know?"

So I pull her over and she straddles me again. I push my fingers through her hair, and it gets tangled in the mass of curls, so I start to massage her head, wondering how I'm going to get my fingers out of the mess and onto her breasts, which I still really want to touch.

Then she tilts her head way back and moans, "That feels so good!"

My heart kind of jumps up. It feels so good to make her feel good. I keep working my fingers on her scalp, slowly pulling them down. I lean in and kiss her neck and then just stay there smelling her. She moans again, and then her hands are in my hair. She starts pulling at it from the back, making me realize how long it's got. It does feel good.

She looks down then and starts to talk, but it takes me a minute to register the words because all I can feel now is her hands in my hair and her hips gyrating on me, grinding over me—hurting so good again, but more hurt now, I think. Is it supposed to hurt so much?

"...I don't know if you have, but..."

"What?" I ask, trying to focus.

"I said I haven't had sex yet and that I want to with you but that I think we should wait. And that I don't know if you even want to."

"Um, yeah, I want to, Michelle," I say sarcastically,

pushing up into her with my boner despite the pain.

"Oh, okay, but shouldn't we wait?" She asks. And it is so sweet. She actually sounds worried.

"You and Jasper never?" I ask and then feel like a loser for asking.

"No," she says, backing off a little, which is what I didn't want to happen. "He wanted to, but..."

"Wants to," I say, correcting her.

"Well, so what? I don't. He's great. He's cute, funny, smart, and I've known him all my life, you know?"

"No, I don't know. So as the new kid, I'm at the advantage?" I ask.

"You could say that," she says, coming in again for a kiss. We kiss, and I can feel her tongue, and then I remember her mouth on me earlier, and I start to kiss her back, like I haven't done in a very long time.

When the kiss and the painful grinding is done, she leans down and snuggles into my neck. I will my heartbeat to slow down.

"I can feel your pulse here," she says, moving her hand under where her face was. She keeps her fingers on my neck and looks up at me. I feel oddly close to her as she feels my heartbeat with her fingertips.

Chapter 14: The Day After

Saturday morning the house is quiet, everyone else is still sleeping, and I have a shit-grin I can't wipe off my face. For the first time in a long time, I don't need my morning ritual. I just get up and want to go. But where? Where can I go in this town? The library, though appealing on one level, is really the last place I want to be this morning. Oh, hey, Lucinda, hell of a mouth on that little lady of yours... he he he... Nope, I should really avoid the library.

I look at the barless flip phone lying by my bed and just kick it under the bed. Not like I need to be tied to Trenton anymore anyway. The best option seems to be the roof, so I lift the window to a cold, bright day, grab my blanket off my bed, and push myself over to the post office roof. I stay low and try to tread lightly to not disturb anyone. I sit down and wrap my blanket tightly around me, wishing Michelle was here.

And then she is. Like I can't believe all this time in Eagle Peak I never realized this before, but she must come to work with her mom on Saturdays because I hear her voice and Lucinda's—they are talking about... books, hmm, there's a shocker.

"But I want to read Harry Potter this morning. The kids would love it!" She is saying.

"No, Michelle. No is no! It isn't appropriate," her mom says.

"What's not appropriate?" I smile listening to Michelle's question. Harry Potter sounds good to me. Does she read to the kids at the library?

"Well, now," says Lucinda. "For starters it has witches!" she says "witches" in a whisper, but loud enough to carry up to the roof for me to hear. "We're not going to discuss this now. Just no. No is no!"

And then keys jingle, the door opens, and they go inside. It must be ten o'clock. The library is open. I sit there a little longer, and am startled when I hear a tap next to me. I turn to my window and my mom is there, waving at me to come in.

I go back in and trudge to the bathroom past where she sits waiting for me at the kitchen bar. I pee, but as I'm doing my final shake I realize it kind of hurts a little—my balls. I look down at my penis. It still looks the same, but it feels so different somehow. It was in her mouth! Oh, Michelle's beautiful mouth. When will I see her again? I could see her now, just go down—check out the self-help books. Ha ha.

Zipping up carefully, I walk out and take a seat beside my mom, still smiling.

"So," she says, smiling back expectantly.

"So?" I say.

"Come on, spill it!"

"Spill what?" Does she know?

"Oh, God, Sean!" she whispers, running her finger along her temple but still trying to smile. I love this game. I could go on for hours, but torturing my mom isn't what I desire to do now. I desire to see Michelle. So I will give her the basics, go see Michelle in the library, make a date to see her after work, and then have a lovely rest of the day.

"I had a nice time, okay? It was a nice dance, and Michelle is a nice girl."

"Yeah, okay, I get it. You don't want to talk to me. Let me just say that today is a meeting at the Hopkins', and I really want you to come with me."

I raise one eyebrow.

She raises one back. "Just one hour of your time. It's good for you to chant, and I know you like it. I do."

"Okay," I say. I will make it back to go see Michelle and then I won't be bugging her at work.

My mom pushes up from her chair. "Let's go then. Gongyo—prayers—starts at 10:30."

She doesn't even knock when we get there. She just walks right in, slips off her shoes, and begins up the steps. I stand suddenly frozen in the doorway just listening to the drone of the chanting. How can I be such an idiot? I didn't even think about the fact that I am entering the home of a girl I kissed, who cried and who denied me based on her skewed view of my sexuality. My mom doesn't turn as I thought she would and urge me to follow. She just keeps walking and disappears. Should I turn around and leave? But then again Lara might think I am running away from her, and I'm not, so I tug off my Chucks and walk into the living room. Everyone but Lara and my mom turn as I come in, smiling at me while they chant. I sit down beside my mom as far from Lara as possible.

Gongyo goes on and on. Reading the sutra book as they rattle it off becomes unbearable, and I find myself nodding off. Then, finally, Daimoku starts, and I am able to join in with the chanting. Nam-myoho-renge-kyo, nam-myoho-renge-kyo, nam-myoho-renge-kyo. It feels good to chant again, and I feel myself wake up a little.

When the chanting is over, I am left with that feeling like it doesn't really feel over, so I just sit there staring at the big wooden box, which Gerald is now closing. Everyone is smiling and moving around, and Lara's parents offer everyone coffee. All the adults leave the room, even my mom.

"You don't really get it, do you?" That's Lara. What the hell she means by that I don't know. "It's good you came."

What am I supposed to say? Nothing.

"I didn't think you would."

I want to tell her I'm not afraid of her, but I'm worried it might come out something like, you clueless girl, you have no idea how much I hate that I kissed you and that you kissed me back and then told me I'm gay, and now you have the nerve to think I'm a wimp. Oh, and by the way, Michelle has better lips than you!

I get up then and leave without saying anything and walk out the door. My mom will figure it out and make her own way home.

I turn down the alley toward downtown, but Lara runs out of the house, and I can hear her feet crunching the gravel to catch up. She grabs my arm and pulls me the other direction. I am annoyed, but I go with her. Why not? "Where are we going?"

"It's a secret place," she says. She doesn't look back.

I run a couple steps to catch up, feeling a little pathetic.

We walk quietly side by side past the junkyard I had walked by on my first day in town, past the little trail leading down to the creek. We walk past a small wood, a field of something. I look up the hill and realize with a jolt that that was where Michelle took me last night. I can see how the trees part a little and how the woods just stops, and then there is a drop down to the road we are walking on. Michelle. The thought of her makes me want to go back, but then Lara turns to the right down another gravel road.

"That's where my mom and I get pussy willows in the spring," she says pointing toward the ditch.

"Pussy willows?" I ask. The name sounds dirty, like it

shouldn't be said out loud in the same sentence as your mother.

"Yeah, they are this plant. They have these little puffs of white fuzz and my mom likes to stick them in vases with other dried plants."

"Huh." What the hell else can I say?

"I am the one that has to pull the branch down and then she saws it off. See, the really good ones grow way up at the top."

Why the hell are we talking about pussy willows? She doesn't seem particularly interested in the topic, but she blathers on and I wonder with a little satisfaction if she is nervous. I just keep walking beside her and wonder what suddenly changed her views of me to grace me with all this intriguing attention.

Then she stops abruptly and claps her hands together loudly.

It is really loud, and I half expect a flock of some kind of bird to go shooting up into the sky. It would top off the scene for sure. I stop too and stare at Lara.

"Let's practice!"

"Practice what?"

"You know, our lines. John and Mina. You have been memorizing them, haven't you? Here, I'll start." She pauses and I keep staring. The way she is acting, it is like she is nervous or something. "Okay, here, 'We've waited this long, haven't we?'"

Jesus, she is serious. What can I do? I take her hand in mine. "We can be married when I return."

"Of course," she grabs my other hand. Her hands are sweaty. So are mine, for that matter. They slip a little and I feel the small muscles and joints in her hand under mine.

"I'll write." I dare her to say the next line—will she say it? The way she is looking at me makes me feel like, well, a man deeply in love just as Jonathan must have felt.

"Jonathan, Jonathan, I love you!" She says it and steps forward.

"I love you, Mina," and then I let her hands drop. Sure, in the script it says we are supposed to kiss, but there is something wrong about doing this the day after Michelle—script or not.

I begin to walk again. "You memorize your lines really well!"

"Yeah, I do. Do you?"

What the hell is she talking about now? I just said them, didn't I? "So what's the big secret you want to show me?"

"I don't know. It's nothing. Maybe we should just go back?"

I shrug, "Okay." I turn to walk back.

Bait taken, she says, "No, I want to show you this. Just follow me."

I follow.

Then she points across a ditch that has patches of snow and dried grass. "We cross here." And then she jumps down into the ditch, sinking into the wet a little, squeals and runs up and over the other side. "Come on!"

I run down, and avoid squealing as my feet sink into questionably wet ground. It's a really cold wet. When I can see over the other side of the ditch, the car junkyard is below us.

"Almost there, Sean. This is my secret place now, so you better be impressed."

Then she starts running between cars. I follow her and understand the need to run since the ground is wet, soft, and cold, and if I stop too long, my feet sink in. We pass whole cars, car parts, broken windshields, and then we stop suddenly in front of a big pink Cadillac. It is totally rusted and old looking, but it is way cool, and pink.

Lara jumps up onto the hood making it groan and

creak and then sits, leaning back against the windshield. She looks at me, and pats the hood beside her. I get up and sit beside her and the hood gives a little more. I wonder if there is even an engine under here.

It feels familiar to be sitting next to her again and reminds me of our first, well, last, kiss. I can't really imagine what the hell she wants to do with me. It doesn't matter that she's giving me that look. She's given me that look before, and that, well, sucked.

"So, you went to the cities?" she asks.

The cities. God, I hate it when they call it that. "Minneapolis. I went to Minneapolis," I said, knowing I sounded like an ass, but who would want to be lumped together with St. Paul?

"Oh, sorry, yeah. Minneapolis. Look, I can tell you're like mad, but you know," and then she drifts off. So I wait. I'm not going to let her off.

"Do you have a girlfriend there? In Minneapolis?" She says Minneapolis sarcastically, which makes me smile a little. So she's mad too. That's good. And she asked, what? Do I have a girlfriend? That's kind of good too.

"No," I say, totally calm, and I can't say I have a girlfriend here either since Michelle and I didn't really talk about that.

"Oh, I just was wondering because you like kissed me and I wasn't sure if you did..." again the drift. And I can understand why. She is totally babbling. And I think in a movie, I would kiss her now. I would stop her from talking and we would make out on the hood of this rusted pink Cadillac. But that's a movie, and we are just kind of awkward and quiet now.

I lean back and wait.

"Oh." She sits there staring at her hands.

I take pity on her awkwardness. There is obviously something she wants to say. "Is this the secret place? This car? I like it."

"Me too," she says, and I think she's regretting she brought me here, but then she whips around and grabs me, and I can't think straight. I can feel her hair between my fingers, so I must have lifted my hands, but I can't remember doing it. I can't figure out how she got on top of me either, straddling me as I lean against the windshield, and she is kissing me and I am kissing her back. I can feel her breasts now because my hands are on them, under her coat, squeezing—they are big and they feel so good. I will myself to push her off, but she is so curvy and sexy and on top of me, and hell, what can I do? I keep thinking this is really wrong, so wrong, but now both my hands are on her breasts and she is moaning. I close my eyes, and I can feel Michelle's hips moving on me up and down. Michelle? No, Lara. Shit, shit, shit. I push her off none too gently and just look at her, trying to see her. And she is gorgeous—blonde hair tussled, cheeks pink and her eyes so dark. I just stare, trying to see Michelle there instead, but it's just Lara, perfect, perfect Lara.

"Thank you," she says quietly.

"Thank you?" I ask. What does that mean?

She laughs a little but puts her head down before she speaks. "No, just thank you for giving me another chance. I kind of fucked it up last time."

Yeah, you really did, but I don't say it.

I get up and start walking away. I have to lift my feet quickly with each step because my feet are getting soaked again. Damn, this just sucks!

"Wait," Lara yells and runs after me.

She catches up and we both start running back to the road. We get there and start walking right away, side by side, not talking. We walk that way all the way back to town. I don't know what she is thinking; I just want to get away from her, but I don't have the guts to tell her that, so I let her walk beside me. She stays by my side past the street that goes to her house, and I almost say something.

"I have to get the mail," she says finally pointing down Main Street where we're headed.

"Yeah, okay," I say.

When we get to the library, I'm about to turn down the narrow lane, but she grabs my hand.

I want to pull away, but she just holds tight. "I'm sorry, Sean. I like you, okay? Think about it, please?" She gives me a quick kiss on the cheek, and then she walks away, and I am left alone right in front of the library's huge window. I self-consciously turn and look into the window in time to see Lucinda turning and walking away quickly. She looks mad, but she always kind of walks like that. Could this get any worse?

Given her mother's observation of Lara and I, I decide I should not go in and see Michelle, and I walk down the narrow alley to our door.

My mom is sitting on the couch with her legs up in Dad's lap. He is massaging her feet. "Michelle stopped by," she says without looking at me. This is good news! That means Michelle probably went home early and wasn't in the library to witness or hear about my hand holding with Lara on Main Street.

"I told her you went for a walk with Lara and didn't know when you'd be back," she says.

"You what?" I say too loudly.

Dad and her snap around to look at me now. "You were, weren't you?" she asked. "Out for a walk with Lara?"

"Well, yeah, but..." It's just too much to explain.

My mom stands up then and walks directly up to me. I look at Dad, who shakes his head slightly then looks down. "What's the problem, Sean?" she asks, and I can see by her eyes she is not concerned at all. She is pissed off. Like really pissed off. I don't like her like this. She never gets mad at me, and I don't like it.

"It's not what it looks like."

"You know what, Sean? I am not the one you need to explain to. You need to figure this out. You should really try chanting to figure it out."

"I'm not going to chant right now, mother!" I yell, suddenly mad she is so righteous in her newly found faith.

"Fine, fine. You know what?" she says, throwing up her arms. "I just," and then she stops, looking like she is totally constipated, and the thought almost makes me smile, but I don't. "No, I'm sorry. I don't mean to jump down your throat, but I just don't like you screwing around with girls' feelings. I raised you better than that!"

I know all this, and I don't really want her to go on with the diatribe, so I say, "Okay," walk to my room, and shut the door.

Then I see there's a package on my bed, really just a thick envelope. It's got Trenton's address. I consider waiting, but I don't. I tear into it and pull out a folded notebook page. A bunch of colorful confetti pours out with it. Annoying as always, Trenton doesn't do anything half-ass.

The letter goes on about his life, the cute new barista at the coffee shop he swears is a hangout for gay bikers, the party where he almost got beat up, his dad not letting him go to school with the lavender cords he found at Savers. It ends with, "You are an asshole, but you know that already, don't you. I forgive you anyway. Sarah doesn't, but she's moving on. Come home. I miss you. Trenton"

He really has no idea what an asshole I can be.

Chapter 15: Rehearsal

I spend the rest of the weekend in my room or on the roofs. I don't call Michelle, and she doesn't call me. I don't call Lara, and she doesn't call me. When I get to school Monday morning it is no shocker that neither talks to me. Michelle just keeps her distance, and Lara, though her locker is right next to mine, seems to not need anything out of it all day. That's all good though; it's not like I have anything brilliant to say to either of them. Part of me knows I screwed up, but another part of me feels like the victim here. I wasn't the one to climb in their laps—I was just a passive recipient of their lust. Yeah, right.

After school I am killing time before our first stage rehearsal of the play. I just stand in the hallway staring into my locker long after most everyone else is gone. I think I am looking for something, but I don't know what it is. Michelle first breaks the no-talking rule by walking up to my locker and almost slamming it shut on my left hand.

"Jesus!" I say, snatching my hand away. "What the fuck, Michelle?"

"Yeah, what the fuck, Sean! Two ladies in one weekend—king of the world, aye?" Her eyes flash mad— really mad.

"I wasn't..." I start and realize it sounds lame.

"You were," she responds and starts to walk away.

I grab her arm. "Wait," I say. "Please talk to me."

She turns then. "No, I'm not the one who has to talk." Then she just stares, arms folded across her chest, waiting. I notice she's wearing fitted clothes. Could it be the sweat days are over?

"So, yeah, I went for a walk with Lara. She kissed me, and then I stopped it because I kept thinking of you," I point at her to clarify. She glares. "We didn't like say we were exclusive or anything, but I want to be." I wait a moment and add, "with you" without pointing this time. Where all that came from, I don't know, but it feels right.

Her eyes narrow. "Are you asking me to be your girlfriend?"

No, not really, but I can't say that. I take a deep breath. "Yes?" I say.

"Okay," she says then bounces up to me and kisses me on the mouth. The change of attitude is too abrupt, and I can't kiss her back in time before she is backing away. "Are you coming? We'll be late."

"Okay," I say finally. "I'm coming." I follow her into the auditorium to our first rehearsal, and again I am struck at its transformation. The seats near the front are filled with students looking up at the elevated stage, and it does look like a stage now. The thick, velvet curtains, which are normally pushed into the corner of the basketball court are pulled around into a U-shaped arc, creating a stage front, two side stages for entering, and a backstage. There are more curtains ready to move across the stage to close it off. I imagine a standing ovation only to open again to me bowing. I remember Lara's dance to the Flaming Lips and imagine how much more impact it would have had with the curtains drawn.

Michelle and I sit together in the front row. Lara walks in a few minutes later and, to my horror, sits down on the other side of me.

I imagined a lot of things when we moved to Eagle Peak. An awkward situation where I am looking at a stage, curtains down, sitting between a girl who just three days ago gave me a blowjob and a different girl who I made out with two days ago on a rusted out pink Cadillac was not one of them.

"Okay, folks," Halestrom says, clapping her hands three times. "It is time to do this thing. I will assume you have all memorized your lines, so if that's not the case, well, let's just say, I will be very disappointed."

"Ooh," I hear his familiar voice behind me, whispering but still clearly Todd's. "Wouldn't want to disappoint you, Mrs. H."

I see a hand pull the back of Lara's hair, and she turns around, clearly annoyed as people laugh around us at Todd's oh so clever joke.

Halestrom looks down to glare at our section.

"Jonathan, Jakov and Innkeeper's wife, come on up." I shuffle up the stairs, happy to be out of that seat between Lara and Michelle. Jasper comes up too as the innkeeper. I can't really imagine a worse part, but that's what he gets for following Michelle around just to, what had he said? Oh, yeah, get in her pants. And then I'm wondering, smiling, if she ever gave him a blowjob. Halestrom nods at me, and I realize I'm up, so I take a deep breath, try to channel Jonathan, boring and reliable Jonathan, and start.

"My name is Harker, Jonathan Harker. I believe you have a room for me?"

Later during a break, I sit down on the stage to keep my distance from Lara and Michelle, who are now all buddy-buddy down in the pit going through costumes.

"So... you and Michelle?" I hear Jasper's voice behind me. He doesn't sit down beside me though—he just stands there.

"Not really," I mutter, craning my neck up to look at him. It's not his business, but I still feel like an ass to basically have taken his girlfriend—the girl he's known all his life.

"Not really? Not really? Do you see her staring at you?" He says, clearly enraged.

I look down and see both girls looking over at us.

Jasper continues in a whisper. "We might not be together now, but don't fuck with her, okay?"

"Can you be more specific?" I ask sarcastically.

"A few weeks ago I actually thought you were cool," he says and walks away, toward the costumes.

Halestrom claps her hand like a spaz, and yells, "Okay, folks, let's take our places. Scene two—Jonathan and Dracula." She says Dracula while sticking out her front teeth and breathing like Darth Vader. It's just embarrassing, but Todd jumps up on stage and hisses back at her. She smiles at Todd and I. "Okay, boys."

Todd stands center stage and pretends to open a door. "Welcome to my house. Enter freely and of your own will. I am Dracula. I bid you welcome, Mr. Harker." He bows a little and flourishes his arm. It is way over the top, but before I have a chance to say my line, there is hooting and clapping from the audience. Basically the entire football team is standing up in the very back row cheering. I hear a "All right, Todd!" And a "You go, Dracula!" Were they like crouched down back there the whole time waiting for Todd's line? What a bunch of losers!

"Wait, wait, wait," Mrs. Halestrom comes out on stage squinting to see them. "You young men cannot be here disturbing our practice."

"Sorry, Mrs. H.," Luke yells. "Can't we just watch?

141

We got so caught up in Todd's performance. We kind of got," and then he pauses. "Overcome," he yells out.

Mrs. H. smiles and shakes her head. "You can stay. But one more peep out of you and you are all out. Maybe it's good to have an audience."

The whole thing is wrong. It makes me want to quit. I didn't join this play to be accosted by the football team. No, they can't stay. How much more am I supposed to take?

But they do stay, and I say my lines, which now seem incredibly boring compared to Dracula's, but I've got the respectable British accent down, while Todd just sounds like a Dracula parody. He's got his lines memorized though, which frankly shocks me.

Finally the football team leaves, and only Michelle and Lara stay to continue their endless sorting of costumes. Basically, I am alone with Todd because Mrs. H went off to the bathroom. We keep practicing, but it is just ridiculous.

"So I saw this special on Transylvania, and it turns out they sound nothing like The Count on Sesame Street, Todd," I say as we are placing ourselves in the next scene.

This would have been one of my mother's lower moments, but it isn't about filtering at this point. It is about artistic integrity.

It is a pin drop situation. Lara and Michelle are quiet and staring at us over the stage from the pit. Todd is looking down like he is debating his next move. I consider that he may want to hit me again, but I feel safe on stage—this is my territory.

Then he looks up and is smiling—it looks genuine, which catches me off guard, and I can't help but smirk a little.

"I think I saw the same one," he says in a perfect toned-down Germanic accent and then laughs. "But do you think our audience did?"

Before I can laugh with him, Mrs. H comes in and does the spaz clap, and I swallow the laugh and the smile and enter my character.

After the rehearsal, Michelle bounces up to me and says, "You were great." I notice that her eyes are again lined in black. She's so damn cute. I feel pretty good about the rehearsal, and I want to kiss her, but I'm kind of shy about it. Especially since Lara is still looking through costumes down in the pit.

"Let's go," I whisper, grabbing her hand and running out the back gym door.

"Oh, Jonathan," she says laughing, "You do the darndest things!"

Not even close to the script, but so what. I'm smiling too as I pull her out the door of the school and start running down the stairs to the sidewalk. At the sidewalk I stop. Our hands are vacuumed together with sweat. It reminds me of Lara's slender, wet hand, but I push that thought out of my head, and lean down to kiss Michelle. She does that hair pull thing in the back again that makes my knees kind of wobble, so I pull her in close for support more than anything, and she moans. I figure getting naked on the front lawn of the school might be considered a PDA, so I break away, and start to pull her home, hoping like hell my parents aren't there.

"Wait," she says. "My car is here."

"Oh, well, let's go get it and go to my place," I say hopefully.

"Yeah, okay," she says. "I have to stop by the library anyway and check in with my mom."

"Right," I say. God, I hope I don't have to be a part of that!

As we get closer to the school lot, we hear a man yelling and pick up our speed.

Turning to see the lot around the school, we can see Todd cowering in front of a tall guy in a suit. He is taller than Todd, but not as beefy. In that brief moment I recognize him—it's the man who swore at the game when Todd dropped the ball. Before I can watch more, Michelle is pulling me back so we can't be seen.

"What, you think you could hide this from me? You worthless cunt!" The voice is booming and much less slurry than it was at the game, but it is scary anyway.

"Todd's dad," Michelle whispers, pointing forcefully around the corner lest I not catch on.

"Got that," I say, annoyed.

I start walking and Michelle grabs my coat. "You can't go out there," she whispers. "He's a grade A asshole and dangerous!"

"Got that too," I say, but hell, am I going to just let this go on and hide and hear? This is what Luke and Lara were referring to, and a lot of good it did them knowing. Maybe it is time someone actually did something.

I shake off Michelle and walk out, clearing my throat loudly. The dad snaps his head toward me and glares, eyes narrow slits like they do in the close-ups of Jackie Chan before a good fight scene. Is this guy for real? My stomach kind of flips, but I fake oblivion. "Hey, Todd, umm, Mrs. H. needs to see you."

Todd doesn't look relieved. In fact, he looks mortified, and I wonder if this is a really bad idea.

His dad is the one who responds by barking out a loud coughing laugh. "Yeah, Todd, go run to Mrs. H." Then he walks to a car and drives off.

I don't walk closer, sure that Todd is going to kick my ass now for seeing all that. I just stare at Todd who is looking down.

"Hey, Sean." It's Michelle, sounding a little too casual. "Come on, we're late."

I nod silently and get into her car with her.

It's a block before either of us speak. "That was cool of you to stop that," she says.

"Mmm," I mumble.

We walk into the library hand in hand. I try to pull away once we're inside, but she has this steel death grip thing going on, and I figure this must be delayed punishment, so I suck it up. She marches right up to her mom who jumps a little when she turns from her shelving to see us.

"Oh, my, you startled me!" she says, one hand on her chest. Then she sees our hands, and her eyes narrow. She looks up at me with what can only be considered a glare then over at her daughter and raises her eyebrows.

I pretend not to notice Michelle's shrug and try to pull my hand away, but Michelle's still got the steel grip.

"Just checking in, Mom," Michelle says. "We're going upstairs to practice our lines, okay? I'll be home for dinner."

"Okay..." Lucinda says skeptically. "Are Sean's parents home?"

"I'm sure they are," I say. Please don't be, please don't be, please don't be....

I smell the garlic as soon as we start up the stairs to my place. No shocker when we walk into the living room still hand in hand and we see my mom at the stove swaying to Cab Calloway.

"Wow," Michelle says and lets go of my hand. My mom turns just as Michelle goes bounding into the kitchen and starts to dance a little. "This is great music! Who is it?"

"Cab Calloway," I say. "A staple for Mom."

My mom is smiling and watching Michelle dance. I can tell she is a little surprised. She is used to Trenton's random behavior, but I don't think she expected it here.

"I do love Cab," my mom finally says and goes back to swaying at the stove and stirring something.

"My parents just listen to country," says Michelle, looking back at me.

I smile a little and keep watching them. They talk comfortably. My mom even gets her to cut veggies. I am largely ignored as I sit on a bar stool watching, bored. I consider getting up a couple times, but I stay, hoping Michelle decides she wants to go to my bedroom to study our lines. She doesn't. She notices the time, says something about dinner at home, and flits out the door.

My mom watches my face after she leaves. "So you two are..." she starts.

"I don't know," I say, turning on the stool.

"By the way, the Hopkins invited us for Gongyo tonight. I'd like you to come."

"I don't know," I say again. No way in hell is what I want to say.

"Just come. Janine mentioned that it will just be her and Gerald, so I assume Lara won't be there."

"Fine," I say, pushing away from the bar.

Chanting at the Hopkins is actually just fine. Without Lara there, I can concentrate and it doesn't feel awkward. I'm able to do a few pages of the book part at the Hopkins speed, but I still like the repetitive chanting part best.

Janine, who is leading tonight, turns in her spot when we are done and hands out an article. "The Ten Worlds: Chief Priest Lecture" it says at the top. She reads it out loud, and I don't really listen, but in the end, when Janine asks us what the lower six worlds are, I look down to focus on the paper.

"Hell, hunger, animality, arrogance, humanity, and rapture," I say.

"Great," praises Janine and my mom smiles and nods.

"Yeah, I'm brilliant! I can read subheadings!" Ugh, I hate patronizing adults. And then I regret it because my mom is glaring now and Janine is quiet and looking down.

Gerald thankfully jumps in. "We like to elevate our life condition beyond the lower six worlds or realms, but it is where we usually operate."

I look down and read under the subheadings a little, especially humanity because isn't that what people are endlessly talking about as the ultimate goal for humans? "Why is humanity one of the lower worlds?" I ask.

"That is a great question, Sean," Gerald says. "From what I understand it is one of the lower worlds because it doesn't change your own or help others change their karma. It just feels good to get along, but it isn't always what we need."

"We don't need to always get along?" I look at my mom and raise an eyebrow. "Did you hear that, Mom? I don't really have to get along with people."

Janine chuckled a little. "That's not what we are saying, Sean, and you know it."

I smile too but look down.

Janine goes on. "It just means that sometimes people have to do what isn't socially acceptable in order to change our karma. For example, in the time of slavery, if they went along with the laws and social norms of that time, we would never see change. It took some people to see beyond the social norm and question it to be able to work for freedom."

Oddly, this makes sense to me. It is a nice concept. They go on to talk about the four higher worlds, but I am stuck on humanity, and on the fact that I certainly go against many of the social norms of this school and this town. If I were to just try to fit in, I would lose myself. I wouldn't be me, and I guess two years of putting up with shit from everyone is better than losing myself.

So it is my green skinny jeans and black tee with my black suit jacket I'm strutting in the next morning through the sea of blonde, which I'm still tripped about. I get to the third floor hall and turn to see Lara and Todd standing by my locker. Nothing odd there, but the how they are standing is new. Lara has both hands on his shoulders and is practically pushing him against her locker, almost aggressive. She is blocking him as I continue my walk toward them. I figure I saved him from a public beating yesterday, so maybe he won't mind me being around.

I couldn't be more wrong. As I get close enough to see around Lara, I can see his face glaring down at her, and he looks worse than I looked when he beat on my face. It is clear he was hit, repeatedly or hard at least, in the face. The reddish-blue and black and cuts are obvious and fresh. I stop, every muscle in my body tense. I want to walk away and not think that maybe I had something to do with this.

Lara turns toward me and nods slightly. She looks back at Todd, who is still staring at me. Her hands go up to his face, and she turns his head toward hers.

"You have to go to the office and report this," she says, and I stand there like an idiot, staring.

He glances back at me and says nothing.

"Todd," she says more loudly. "This is too much!"

"Now it's too much? Why? 'Cause you can see it?" Todd snarls and shoves her. I put a hand on her back so she doesn't fall, and he walks away—head up, ignoring the stares.

Lara kind of leans into my hand, and when I see her eyes, there are tears.

"I did this," I say, needing to confess to someone.

"You did?" She says, surprised.

"Yeah, I stopped his dad from kicking his ass yesterday in the school parking lot, but it must have made him madder or something. I don't know."

"Oh, Sean, you just don't get it," she says like I'm the biggest fucking idiot in the universe. "This so isn't about you." And then she turns and walks away.

And I am an idiot, of the biggest kind. Michelle bounces up and puts a hand in my pocket.

"Mmm, green skinny jeans. That's hot," she whispers into my ear, biting a little.

But I'm not in the mood and I step away.

"I gotta go," I say as I walk away.

I don't even bother to turn around.

The week goes on. The practices go on. The football team stops coming after a couple days and this is a wonderful thing. We get through the whole play twice in the week. Outside of our time on stage, Michelle and I don't talk a whole lot. We're busy, I guess.

But Friday her flop of red hair pushes up between me and my locker, and this time I don't back away but rather lean in for a kiss. And we're kissing and I kind of lose myself; we are half in my locker when I hear a familiar voice behind me, Jen's.

"Well, well," she says. "Sean, I don't know how they do things in the cities, but around here we try to refrain from PDA."

I pull away from Michelle and turn and am faced by not just Jen, but Lara too, who is trying not to look at anyone.

"We fuck in the hallways at South, Jen," I say while staring at her. It's the cold glare.

"Come on, Jen," Lara says and pulls her friend down the hall.

I feel Michelle's arms go around my waist. "Really?"

she says into my back. "You all fuck in the halls?"

"No," I say staring down the hall after Lara.

"Hey," Michelle says, kind of shaking me so I turn. "There's a party tonight—Dan's house."

"Not a ditch party?" I ask, still distracted.

"No, smartass. There'll be a bonfire. His parents will be around, but it's always fun anyway."

"Okay."

"I'll pick you up," she says.

"Okay," I say.

Chapter 16: Drinking Blood

It's not the animal ditch party scene I expected. We park Michelle's mom's car off to the side of the drive-way, but the huge fire across the lawn and the people milling about strikes me as yet another unique situation I am in for here. I flip the mirror down in Michelle's car to take a quick look as she parks.

"Shit, I forgot liner!" I can't believe I forgot. I am getting hick. This realization makes me want to write Trenton—crap, I forgot to write Trenton.

"I've got some," she says. She pulls out a tube of black liquid liner from her backpack.

"I'm not so good with the liquid stuff."

"I can do it," Michelle says, already sliding over to me.

I wince a little. "What if you screw up?"

"I won't," she says smiling as she straddles my lap. She's wearing jeans, which is a bummer in this situation. She is also wearing a sweatshirt—not a huge one though. She opens the tube and wiggles her eyebrows at the slurpy sound it makes then leans in. "Look up," she says. Her breath smells like peppermint.

I can tell she knows what she is doing, and this takes talent since my hands are slowly sliding up her pants, over her soft belly skin toward her boobs. By the time she is done with both eyes, I have both hands over both boobs.

"Okay," she says, "Look at me."

I slide my hands down as I look at her.

"God, there is something really sexy about putting eyeliner on your boyfriend."

Yeah. Funny. As if. "I'm thinking you would be in the minority on that account." I start sliding my hands back up, and she lets me.

She pushes down on me then and kisses me at the same time, and suddenly the bonfire is infinitely less interesting than it had been.

"Hey, horndogs," I hear as someone's face smashes into my window. It's Lindsey. Michelle laughs and rolls it down.

Lindsey smiles at me. "Hey."

"Hey," I say. So we are back at the hey stage now.

Dan is lingering behind Lindsey, and kind of nods when I look at him. I nod back, open the door, and pour Michelle off my lap.

She gives Lindsey a big hug and starts talking quietly with her. I walk over to Dan and stand there. I don't know what he's thinking, but I'm sure I'm on his shit list. I wonder if Jasper is coming. I also wonder if they all wish I just never came to their town.

Dan finally says something. "First bonfire?"

"Yep," I say.

"We do this every year—my parents' friends come, and I get to invite my friends. Usually, most of the school shows up by the end of the night."

"They don't mind?" I ask.

"No, but they also don't allow any drinking."

"Makes sense," I say.

"Yeah, but everyone shows up drunk anyway," he says, smiling a little.

"We didn't." For some reason I want to try. It's not like Dan and I have anything to talk about, but he was one of the first people to actually talk to me, and I feel like I owe him.

He hands me his can of Coke. "Try this."

I look at it. Normally, I hate sharing germs, but hell, I am trying, right? And I take a swig, and then almost spit it out and gag.

"What is that?" I gasp.

"Vodka and Coke," he smiles.

I don't give it back and take another drink, a bigger one. It's bad and kind of good too.

"Whatcha got there?" Michelle asks as she skips over to us.

"Just Coke," I say about to take another sip, but she grabs the can out of my hand and takes a swig.

"Mmm," she moans. "Dan's Coke. Thanks, man!" and she takes another gulp.

"Um, yeah, great to make you all happy, but could I have my Coke back?" Dan asks.

Michelle hands it back and giggles. She can't possibly be tipsy yet. But even my fingers feel a little tingly.

We stand around and talk about the play a little, well, Michelle talks. She is hilarious, acting out her scenes like a freak. I join her when I can.

Overall, it is a pleasant time. Until Jasper shows up. He gets out of his car all morose and depresso. Suddenly we are all awkward and quiet.

"Well, should we go?" I ask, feeling beyond awkward.

"Go? Why?" Michelle looks over at Jasper, then back at me, and tries to smile.

She knows why, but I explain the obvious anyway. "Because I don't feel like I should be here."

"It's not all about you, Sean," Michelle says, parroting Lara's earlier comment. But it is, of course. I'm all I really know.

Michelle leaves me and walks toward Jasper. They stand by his car talking quietly.

"It's getting cold, huh?" Lindsey says and then looks right at me. "Gone home recently?"

Home. She called Minneapolis home. Yep, they definitely want me out of here. "No, not in a few weeks. It's about time though."

"Let's go check out the fire, Linds," Dan says. They walk away. Dan has his arm around Lindsey, rubbing her arm to warm her up.

I stand there for a while, trying not to look at Jasper and Michelle, who are now seeming to have a pretty heated discussion. I turn and walk back to Michelle's car to sit down. I so want out of here, but I have no idea where I am, so walking home isn't an option. I guess I just have to sit and wait for my "girlfriend" to give me a ride.

In her car, I roll up the window. I'm getting cold too, and I rub my hands up and down my thighs wishing I had keys to at least put the heater on. I look around the car. It smells like Michelle's farm—corn and poop. I wonder then why Dan's place doesn't smell like that. It's out in the country. Maybe they just keep things cleaner. Then I notice Michelle's flute in its case laying on the back seat. I lean back and grab it, open it, and try to put it together the way I remember from 5th grade instrument introduction. Putting my hands on the keys I blow. A sound actually comes out, a flute sound. It sounds nothing like when Michelle plays it. I keep playing around with it until Michelle opens the door and sits down beside me.

"No, keep going," she says when I bring her flute down.

"I don't know what I'm doing," I say.

"Well, that's clear enough, but you know what they say about practice."

"I'd rather hear you play," I say handing it to her.

She takes the flute and begins pulling it apart. "Later," she says.

"So, is everything okay?" I ask, trying to sound like a supportive boyfriend. Jesus, what am I doing here? It's like I have to feed myself lines.

"Everything is fine," she says getting back out of the car. "Let's go."

I follow even though I don't want to.

The whole scene is completely tripped out. There is the fire, which is the obvious oddity with its flame as tall as two of me. It is wide and there are like tree-sized logs on the bottom. There's also random garbage, and do I see a shirt in the fire too? Then there are the adults, sitting on thick logs and lawn chairs, staring into the flames and talking in low murmurs, largely ignoring the kids except for the creeper variety of men checking out the young ladies. The kids are either standing around talking, their eyes locked on the dancing flames, or they are running about chasing each other, and some occasionally walk off to a car, presumably to make out. Michelle tells me the music is Garth Brooks, a "classic at these events."

Michelle and I stand close to the fire to keep warm. She doesn't touch me at all, and I don't wonder why. Jasper stands apart from us, glaring. I can't imagine a more unpleasant use of my time, frankly.

Finally, Michelle sidles up to me. "Got anything against KC and the Sunshine Band?"

"Um, no, should I?"

"Well, I got this tape in the car, and I think it is a happy medium for the kids and adults," she says, and I smile a little at her wisdom.

She reaches up then to touch my face. "You do look nice when you smile." Then she walks off toward the car, and I stand, feeling the glares from Jasper and watching the flames lick the cold black night air.

She comes back to the fire and walks to the boom box. Turning off Garth produces a series of shouts from the adults, but she seems to take it easily. "Come on, we need something a little livelier."

"Who needs music, little lady? I got all the lively I need right here," one of the adults yells. I watch him grab his crotch and sway a little when he stands, and then with great pleasure I watch him get slapped in the head by an older woman; it must be his wife.

Michelle ignores the comments and presses play, and "Boogie Shoes" comes out blaring. I smile as she saunters my way and appease her by taking her one outstretched hand and spinning her. And for a long while it is just the two of us dancing, trying to do a partner dance and failing miserably. By the end of the song, though, some of the adults are out two-stepping or whatever they do in line dances, and other teens are hopping about. Lindsey has joined us and is dancing poorly, but Michelle enthusiastically incorporates her into our dance, and we become a circle. When she begins her version of disco, I can hold back no longer and I raise one arm in a pump and cross the circle in my best horse trot. Then, in my little world, the zone is hit and I am lost in disco rapture.

Michelle is as insatiable a dancer as I am, and we outlast everyone. As the adults drift off, she gets a new tape, Bob Marley, and a slower grinding dance begins. By this time most of the kids are drunk on spiked pop—there must be some kind of center of vodka-Coke production and refill because Michelle and I are handed by random kids two full cans of Coke of the vodka variety. I vaguely notice the fire is dying out, but I'm not cold at all because between the alcohol and the dancing, I am actually sweating. Michelle is sweaty too, so when "Three Little Birds" comes on, I grab her, put my hands under her shirt, and she shivers as my cold hands slide up her wet back. We stay that way, our hips mashing into each other, swaying back and forth, and our arms slipping all over the place under the bulk of our shirts. I think we are both too drunk for coordination, but not too drunk to get excited, so by the time I pull her toward her car as "Buffalo Soldier" blares out, she is pulling me too.

We slam down onto the back seat and start grinding immediately, but then the coldness of being away from the fire and not dancing settles in and we are shivering, and I realize there is no way in hell I will be getting her naked in this car unless we put the heat on.

"Heat," I croak.

"Okay," she says. "Just a sec."

Then she slides up over the front seat. I can tell she hits her head on the steering wheel twice, but I don't think she notices. She just laughs and giggles and turns the key.

It's still cold though as she slips back into the seat with me.

"Take your shirt off," she says.

"Are you nuts?" I say, genuinely concerned now for her sanity. It is cold. "You first."

So she pulls off her sweatshirt, and unlatches her bra, letting the straps hang. She is daring me. And who am I not to oblige? I start unbuttoning my dark grey dress shirt. The cold air hits my chest hard, but just as I am about to complain, she pulls off the bra the rest of the way, and those wide soft breasts land on my chest creating the most splendid feeling. Splendid, definitely a Jonathanism. "Skin to skin is the best way to warm up," Michelle says. Yeah, whatever. I would believe anything she told me at this moment.

She leans down and starts to do some kind of biting sucking thing on my neck which kind of hurts but also kind of feels good. I lean in to do the same to her and she leans her head back, and it makes me feel good to know this is what she does when she is really feeling it. I lick her salty neck and then I bite a little. Her hips grind down

157

on me, and then I bite harder and start to suck. I might as well make this a proper hickey, and since I've never given one before I err on the side of too long to make sure the proper marking remains. Just as our tongues dive into each others' mouths, a few sets of headlights start bouncing, throwing light throughout the car.

"Latecomers," she murmurs as she settles in for another kiss.

It seems I am more distracted by the incoming cars than she is, but when the shouts and hoots erupt as car doors open, reality sets in for us both, and she grabs her sweatshirt and slips it on quickly without a bra. I button my shirt and pull my jacket tighter just in time before the car starts bouncing due to two large creatures jumping on the hood of her car.

"Football players," she says with a groan.

"Ya think?" Why the hell is it that I can't just have sex with a girl like normal guys do? I mean, is it too much to ask that I have my first sex before the age of eighteen? I would like to get good at it before college!

We bounce out of the car and are surrounded by what looks to me like the entire football team. Michelle is undaunted. "Get the FUCK off my car!" she screams at the two oafs still jumping.

"Look, Michelle," says who I now recognize as the psycho pisser. "We don't have an issue with you. We have an issue with this faggot here," he says pointing to me.

"Faggot?" Michelle squeals. "Faggot?" she asks again for effect. "What the fuck are you talking about? He is neither a pile of sticks nor a gay man. In fact, we were on our way to having some hot sex if you hadn't so rudely interrupted!"

I am stuck on the pile of sticks reference and her lack of fear of saying the word gay. The hot sex was assumed by me too, and I am oddly ambivalent about that. She isn't afraid of anything—not football players, not being intelligent, not gayness. I am suddenly feeling proud to have such an amazing girlfriend.

Until Luke walks out into the center of the circle that has formed around us. "He's just leading you on," he says straight-faced to Michelle.

"Leading me on?" she says, "Does this hickey look like he is leading me on? And he seemed willing enough...."

I can tell where she is going with this, so I grab her arm before she divulges my twenty second blowjob. "Luke, can we just talk about this?" I ask. I can be reasonable. I sadly understand what is motivating this guy more than he himself does.

"No," he says and steps forward toward me, hands clenched.

"I don't want to fight you," I say. I don't say "I can't" which is more the truth.

"Of course you don't," he says glancing around to his friends, "because you are a faggot!" At this a few of the guys chuckle.

I am beginning to panic now. I don't see any way out of this other than getting my ass kicked. And when that's been done, I imagine the torture will continue. How could it not? I take a step back away from Luke, and Michelle tries to step between us. Luke pushes her aside and steps in again, staring at me and shaking. "I hate you," he says.

"No, you don't," I whisper. *You hate yourself*, I want to say, but I can't muster a voice. I've never felt this sinking fear before. I tense, ready to fly at him and know that I will get bloodied tonight. The other football jocks circle in tighter.

"Whoa, kids!" The adult-like words are coming out the mouth of my other enemy. He saunters into the circle and puts a hand on Luke's shoulder. Luke shakes it off, not taking his eyes off of me.

"Hey, Luke," Todd says urgently. He says it like he is trying to pull Luke back from the verge of death. He then starts to talk, softly and intently, about football, about Luke's family, about me, about me not being gay, about it being a mistake. I've never heard Todd's voice this way, so soft and calm. I wonder if this voice would work on his dad?

Luke's body slowly softens, but I stay tense and ready. Todd claps his hands then and says, "Well, this is lame. Let's go ditchin'!" He starts off and the others follow, heading back to their cars. Luke stays, staring down at the ground. "Luke!" Todd yells, not friendly this time. Luke turns slowly, not looking back at me, and follows the group into a car and they all drive off.

I back up to the car and slump against the cold metal as Michelle glares after everyone—always the good bodyguard. When there is an unblocked way out of the driveway, Michelle starts to get into the car. "Let's get you home," she says.

I can't move though. I can't form words in my mouth.

"Sean!" she yells, much the same way that Todd yelled at Luke. "Home."

My brain registers that she is treating me like a two-year-old, but I don't care. I just follow the instructions and get into the car.

Chapter 17: Kung Fu

I don't remember getting into my bed last night, or getting home for that matter, but I can't seem to make everything that happened before that point stop from playing through my brain like a horror movie I am forced to watch.

Before my mom can invite me to another Buddhist meeting or ask me to breakfast, I formulate a plan for the day—solitary avoidance. I deserve this. The clock reads 10:00 a.m., and I don't hear any noise from the kitchen, so I throw on some clothes and open the door quietly. Then like Bruce Lee my mom springs in front of me, does this laughable karate arm wave in a very awkward squat, and starts talking, deleting but mouthing every other word—years of practice, I guess. Dad, who clearly loves my mom despite her personality, is sitting on the couch giggling. Between the hysterics, I gather that it is Kung Fu Saturday blitz, an event my parents put on at least twice a year. I use the term "event" loosely, as it is typically just my parents, me and Trenton watching every Kung Fu movie they own. We ingest lots of caffeinated beverages, frozen pizza, and popcorn—Trenton and I always get hyper and end up in a living room battle judged by my parents. The thought of those better days hurts now.

"Can't do it, Mom. Not in the mood at all," I say.

Dad leaps from the couch, squats as mom does, and says, "Surely... don't...you...stay... from... kung...

Saturday...It would... lame... very... unsonly."

I try not to because I'm about as pissy as I get, but I let out one small smile. That is all they need. So I walk toward the door, away from the madness.

"Back you will come," Mom yells.

"You're mixing your movie lines, Mom. That's Yoda speak!"

"Aaahh. Mixing... lines... horror... horror," Dad screams, clutching his head. Man, they are on a roll this morning!

As I run down the steps, my mom says, "The horror, the horror..." They can never remember the right Brando lines, but they try.

I have to rearrange my face when I get outside. I'm pissed, uncertain, totally fucked, I remind myself. My face follows my brain, and I got a good scowl on by the time I round to Main Street. And that is how I am looking when I almost crash into Lucinda, precariously balancing three boxes and trying to reach for her keys.

"Oh, Sean, can you just grab these..." she is red-faced and looks very tired, her speech is almost slurring. I wonder for a moment if she is drunk.

I grab the boxes quickly from her, worried she might collapse. They are light—must be paperbacks.

She gets her keys in her hand, but she is shaking so much, she can't even put the key in the lock. There is a long moment where she just stares at her hand as if she is willing it to stop shaking, but there is no control. She really can't do it.

I put the boxes down on the sidewalk and take the keys from her. "This one?" I ask, holding up the key she had in her hand.

She just nods slightly, not looking me in the eyes.

I try not to make a big production out of it as I unlock and open the door, and then follow her in with the boxes.

I quietly put the keys down on the front desk and turn to walk out, assuming she wants to be alone.

She doesn't. "Sean," she says softly, sitting down with a thump at her desk.

"Yes?" Is she going to confess to drugs, alcohol?

"I have MS. That is why I shake and my mouth doesn't work right. It's a flare-up right now. I'm sorry."

My heart kind of breaks because she tells me this like she is confessing to murder. I consider telling her that MS is a lot better than being an addict, which is what I thought she was, but I think better of that, and just look down too. My eyes trace the pattern of the carpet on the floor. Really bad floral, grey background with maroon flowers and dark purple leaves. I imagine nothing like that ever occurs in nature.

"I just thought you should know," she says. Then she slaps her thighs with her hands and pushes up, clenching and unclenching her hands. She starts bustling around, moving the boxes and the keys.

"Can I help you do something?" I ask, not sure what kind of sick MS is. Her eyes finally look at me, and they narrow. Not that kind of sick, I guess. "Not that you need any help. It's just, I am kind of trying to get away from my parents today. They are doing this Kung Fu movie marathon upstairs, which means they are completely obnoxious. I wouldn't mind hanging down here a bit." Of course, this is a lie. This was going to be my day alone. I need a day to think, to sort out everything that has happened. But I can't let go of the nagging feeling that Lucinda shouldn't be alone here, not during a "flare-up," whatever the hell that means.

"Funny, but Michelle said the same thing—that she needed some time away from us all. She took off in the truck—who knows where."

So I stay. Her eyes stop narrowing, and she starts

acting more like the Lucinda I would expect. She orders me around—put these boxes there, arrange these books in alphabetical order after arranging by number, reshelve these. And she complains—about Vicki, the library assistant who works during the workweek and doesn't do anything besides sit and check books in and out. Lucinda has to make up for all the backed up work from the whole week on her weekend shifts. The work is nice, and absolutely no one comes in, but I guess it is still pretty early. It takes me a while to alphabetize. I keep having to sing the ABC's in my head to the letter I am on. I wonder if everyone does this when they put things in alphabetical order. These are the deep thoughts that occupy my mind as I work. And it's work. I'm not getting paid, so I imagine this means I am a library volunteer. That has got to go into the letter I am writing in my head to Trenton. It is impressive, kind of, not like the parties I go to or the sex I almost have with girls here. Not like Jonathan Harker, boring and predictable.

Then Michelle walks in. She doesn't see me at first, but I can see her hair around the shelf I am working on.

"Hey, Mom. Sorry. I'm better now. What should I do, boss lady?" she asks. And I think for the first time that maybe I'm not the only person in the world who has a functional relationship with my parents.

"Well, sure. We've got plenty to do. You know how Vicki is," Lucinda seems happy that someone new is here to complain too.

"Yep. What should I do?"

"Well, you can..." and then she remembers me. "Oh, but I forgot. Sean, come on out."

Michelle whips her head around and stares at me. I can't read what she is thinking. "What are you doing here?" she asks, clearly shocked.

"Just helping out." She is looking at me like this is her

territory. And then I remember everything from last night like a tidal wave of shame. I was scared. Really scared, and Michelle knew it. If it weren't for her and Todd...

I stand absolutely still as she walks toward me. I have an irrational feeling of panic, similar to how I felt with Luke. She walks right up to me, puts one hand on my left cheek and kisses the right one. "Okay," she says and turns to grab more books from the desk. She just walks around the library shelving them. She doesn't need to sort them before reshelving, and she doesn't seem to need to do the ABCs in her head either. She just looks really quick at the book then walks right to where it should go and sticks it in. Effortless, really. After some time, she starts to peek coyly around the corners of shelves, winking like a complete dork. It's cute.

Lucinda suggests we go off and "enjoy ourselves" when our work becomes a series of winks and giggles. She doesn't seem to appreciate our youthful exuberance.

I glance at her hands as we walk out though, and they aren't shaking any more. Must be the end of the flare-up.

I make the mistake of telling Michelle about Kung Fu Saturday Blitz, and she wants to go up. I don't completely mind either even though I would rather go have sex in her truck.

We walk into the living room and my mom says, "Ah, prodigal son returneth!" They are on Gate Palace, a classic, and an early one—we've got a long way to go!

The day is spent on the couch. Michelle stays cuddled up against me, feeling my ass under my pants. I wonder how she is able to get her hands under there, and I wonder how it feels. When I clench my butt cheeks she laughs and squeezes, so I imagine it must feel kind of marshmallowy. I am not sure how to get my hands on her though without my parents knowing. I wonder if they would care, but I would, so I just sit there, dozing off now and then. At one point I wake up and Michelle's head is in my lap. She is tracing lines on my knee and thigh, and I instantly get hard. And embarrassed. My mom and dad aren't there, and I wonder how long we've been like this. Michelle can feel me getting hard, and she turns and looks up at me, giving me a sly smile. I nod at my room, but just then my parents come out of their bedroom. I wonder what they were doing in there.

"Hungry?" my mom asks.

And so the day goes on. And on. And on. And then ends with Michelle going home. I realize then how different it is to have a Kung Fu marathon with Trenton, and I actually think I prefer that to the torture of Michelle's hands all over me with me unable to do anything about it.

Sunday comes with the very predictable announcement by my mother that we are going to the Hopkins'. I go.

We are early, or they are late. Janine invites us in for coffee, but I notice as I peek into the living room that Lara is sitting on the couch, her feet tucked up under her, listening to music. I walk up to her, and she looks up.

"What are you listening to?" I ask.

She pulls out one earbud and hands it to me. I sit right next to her and put it in. It is a smooth woman's voice. Spanish or something—I can never tell when it's singing. Her voice is as deep as a man's and the piano is plunky and sexy. I lean back on the soft couch and close my eyes. I can feel her do the same. Lara's arm is touching mine. We must have drifted off because when I open my eyes, Janine and my mom are staring at us smiling with eyebrows raised, a classic mom look. We both sit up, kind of out of sorts. I pull the music out of my ear.

"Cesaria Evora," Lara says.

I nod. "It's nice."

We all settle on the floor, kneeling in front of the Gohonzon. I am happy that I finally remembered not to wear tight jeans and can kneel comfortably.

I am able to do pages one through four now, and on page four where they repeat a part three times, I can do it without looking. I am oddly proud of this until we get to page five and I have trouble even following along with my finger. At one point I get lost and look over at Lara's book—she doesn't turn but smiles and points to our place on the page. She is just so calm when she is chanting. It's like completely effortless for her and she doesn't need to even think. It reminds me of Michelle shelving books. Then I start to list the things that are effortless to people. Trenton can make anyone laugh, Dad is totally in the zone at his job, my mom is comfortable doing anything new or being a dork, Sarah is just really really cool, Todd can throw and catch a ball with no effort and apparently talk someone down from a rage, the Kung Fu dudes can flip and fly without a thought, and me? I must have something. And then I think again of the monologue I went to state with—I can still feel the spotlight on me, and everything else black. Nothing else mattered but the feelings of the character I played—my body melded into the body of the character and even my voice pitch changed. Yeah, that is my zone. I'm not doing Jonathan Harker any favors—it is time to step up my game and make this character come alive.

The chanting ends and I smile at the realization that I too have a Kung Fu power.

Chapter 18: Many Bodies, One Mind

I'm ready to go before the meeting is over, but Gerald turns and pulls out some paper. It is thick and I almost groan. Study material—I guess Buddhists are into suffering? I take my packet dutifully and read the top, or try to.

"Ita Dosh..." I try to say.

"Itai Doshin," Gerald says smiling. "It is one of the most important concepts in Buddhism."

"Hmm." I am not impressed.

Lara starts to read. I watch her as she reads. She is gorgeous to look at after all, and the way she reads is sweet, kind of slow and clear, like she has to concentrate to get it out right. I try to think about what she is saying rather than how she is saying it, but she is going on and on about one mind and many bodies, and I can't track it.

Then it's my turn to read. "Yet a hundred or even a thousand people can definitely attain their goal if they are of one mind."

"So what does this mean. Lara? Sean?" Gerald is trying in his very adult way to process and draw us into the reading.

"I always wondered about this," Lara starts. "Why do we have to have one mind?"

Gerald and Janine look proudly at their daughter—asking such a great question. I almost roll my eyes, but I kind of wonder too—it sounds a little, I don't know, like

168

you are either with us or against us, so what's it going to be?

"One mind doesn't mean we all think alike," Janine says. "It means we all have the same goal."

"Well, isn't that the same as everyone thinking alike?" I ask.

My mom looks at me in a similar way as Lara's parents are looking at her. They know they've got us and couldn't be more pleased.

Gerald attempts to explain that having a common goal, in this case chanting, is not the same as thinking the same. He talks about race, class and gender being irrelevant in Buddhism—that everyone can attain enlightenment. I am left wondering if he purposely avoided the question. Lara just nods and looks down, squinting at the paper, and slowly reads on.

As we are leaving Lara's house, Todd's car drives down the alley. I think he times his visits to miss these meetings. Hmm, part of me thinks he is brilliant and part of me thinks that he is really dumb to want to miss chanting. Maybe he's afraid, and that thought makes me kind of happy, but remembering how he basically saved me last night pisses me off again.

As my mom and I are leaving, he opens the door. He smiles brightly, and there are still smudges of bruising across his right cheek. "Vell, if it isn't my arch nemesis, Jonathan!"

I want to ask him about his dad, to apologize, but I somehow don't think that is what he wants, so all I say is, "Where's your teeth, Todd?"

"I seem to be growing new teeth. I don't need the fakeys any more. I'm really channeling this character!"

"Hmm," I say. "Method acting?"

"Sure," he says, and slips by us. He gets to the top of the stairs and pulls Lara into a tight hug and kisses her neck. Lara doesn't look like she's not enjoying it, so I guess they are back together then.

My mom and I walk home quietly. I can tell she wants to talk to me, but I don't offer her any openings in my silence, so thankfully, she doesn't ask anything.

Another Monday and things could really suck, but I've got this Kung Fu power to get me through the day. I look forward to Dracula practice—to showing everyone how I can be Jonathan, how I can feel his character. They won't know what hit them.

Luke spends the day avoiding me, not even looking in my direction. The other jocks don't say anything either, but I can tell they see me differently. Perhaps it is Michelle hanging on my arm, in my locker, her hand in my back pocket. It's like a record with her—how many PDAs can we commit. Anyway, it seems to do the trick with the jocks.

After English, I am at my locker, Michelle is in the bathroom, and Lara walks up beside me. I can smell her before I see her. That surprises me. It's not like instant boner kind of smell either. It's just a familiar kind of smell. I turn to her and smile.

She smiles back and pats her hand over her hair covering her cheek.

"Why do you do that?" I ask.

"Do what?"

"Cover your mole," I say.

"Do I?" She touches it then, tracing the mole with her fingertip. "I don't know. Maybe I just... I never noticed."

"I like your mole. I don't think you should cover it," I say, hoping we are friends enough to say this to each other.

We are. She laughs. "I'll work on that, Sean."

After school I walk to the auditorium with Michelle. Since we've only got a week of practice left, the curtains are out, and, I imagine, will stay out all week. We sit in the front row and await Mrs. Halestrom's spastic claps, but much to my horror, Dad enters through the side curtain pushing a cart of power tools in front of him with Mrs. Halestrom close behind.

"Well, we've made it to tech week!" Mrs. Halestrom bellows. Again, the claps.

"The goal today is to make several five by fifteen flats," Dad says, motioning to the pile of wood that I just notice is sitting on the stage. He lifts the power drill up and revs it, and I am fairly mortified now. "How many of you know how to use power tools?"

Pretty much everyone raises their hands. Yeah, as if.

"Okay," he chuckles, "let me rephrase that. How many of you have used power tools in the past?"

A few hands drop, but Todd stands up and jock walks to the stage. "Mr. Anderson, I think I am your best bet with those tools. Just show me what to do."

The practice proceeds in this hideous manner. Todd is strutting around raising the drills up and revving them as Dad had done, Michelle and Lara and some of the other girls are hammering wood together to make the support for the flats, and I am stuck painting flat upon flat in a boring white.

Someone turns on the radio—it is bad pop. I look at everyone now—really look. We look like a team. The girls are all singing and dancing as they hammer—trying to hammer to the beat. The guy playing Helsinki, I don't remember his real name, is dancing alone in the corner in his maroon overcoat, Mrs. Halestrom is walking toward him like she's going to reprimand him for putting on his costume, but then Michelle grabs her and pulls her into a waltz—how she does that, pulling people in to dance, I will never know. She's infectious.

I turn around and try to refocus on painting, but then I hear Dad's laughter and turn in time to see him slapping Todd's back, and Todd beams. I think about Todd's dad, and I wonder if he and his dad have ever worked power tools together. I imagine not. I look away before he sees me watching—I imagine he needs this, and I'm sure Dad loves having an apprentice.

It's all good until it's not. Jasper, my new Todd, is trying out an attitude. And it seems to work. His hair, extra curly and sticking up all over like a mad scientist, seems to be getting the attention of the ladies. Michelle, in particular. He butts in on the waltz and pulls Michelle awkwardly around the stage. Michelle looks at me briefly, but she is smiling as he turns her away, and they waltz on. I just focus in on my work.

Basically, that is how the entire week goes. There is so much to do to get ready for the play this weekend. Again, Michelle and I don't interact a whole lot. It is crazy how hot and cold she is, but I'm not too worried about it.

Friday afternoon I am backstage behind the heavy curtains, fidgeting with my long hat, and waiting. It is quiet. People are tiptoeing around, waiting as the auditorium fills with the students. Everything is set for the school play, the "practice" for the real thing tomorrow. This terrifies me far more than any other stage work I have ever done. In Minneapolis, it is easy to pretend you don't know anyone in the audience because you don't, but here, these are people I will probably be seeing for the next year and a half. Yes, terrified is the right word.

Then the gym door swings open with a bang, and

everyone stops doing what they are doing to watch Mrs. Halestrom storm in, but it isn't Mrs. Halestrom. It is Trenton. And behind him Sarah. And they walk in like they own the fucking school.

Trenton glares around him, finds me, and walks quickly in my direction. I have a hard time reacting at first, and then watching the two of them, Trenton in his sweater vest layered over a button-up under some ugly-ass bib overalls, Sarah in a tight, low-cut shirt and baggin' and saggin' jeans, I am shaken out of my shock and start to dance around on my toes, arms outstretched like an excited two-year-old.

Trenton stops in front of me, pretends to slap me in the face and says, "Jesus Sean, look at you! And you wonder why you aren't fitting in. Get a grip!"

"Oh, shut the fuck up, Trenton," Sarah says, and walks around him, pulls off my top hat with one hand and grabs a handful of hair in the other and pulls me down into a very Sarah kiss. My body remembers and my hands start under her big jeans. I'm not thinking about anything at all. I am just kissing Sarah, and it feels so right. I just pull her in and start shamelessly gyrating.

"Well, isn't this pleasant," Trenton says, and Sarah and I pull away, smile into each other and reach and pull him into our embrace. "There now," he says, "that's better."

We stand like that a while. I suppose I should feel awkward, but I don't. The whole thing just feels right.

"You wore overalls," I say to Trenton through Sarah's hair.

"Well, of course."

Sarah pulls away, looking at her watch. "Let's go, Trent. Sean's got a play to put on."

They turn to go. "Wait!" I yell. "You're staying, right?"

They both roll their eyes. "No, Sean," Sarah says. "We

just drove for three hours for some two-minute lovin'!"

They laugh as they walk away.

I can't stop smiling as they walk out. Even when Mrs. Halestrom comes in right after them, I still stand there smiling like an idiot.

"What the fuck was that?" whispers Michelle.

"What?"

Michelle. Shit. What was I thinking kissing Sarah like that? I wasn't. "Those are my friends, Michelle."

"My friends don't kiss me like that!" she says, too loud now.

"Yeah? But you and Jasper have been getting pretty cozy."

"What?" She says, acting all incredulous. "That was a dance—a fucking waltz. Why didn't you say something? Instead you just try to get me back with a frenchie with your ex?"

"I wasn't thinking of you, Michelle," I say, knowing it would hurt.

Halestrom starts some weird silent spaz-clapping. "Come on folks," she yells in a whisper. "Places!"

Michelle glares at me as I shrug. I grab her hand. Mine is sweaty. "Break a leg," I say.

"You break a fucking leg, Sean."

And then she huffs off and everyone is moving again; the shift makes me realize that everyone has been waiting for something else to happen, as if Trenton and Sarah were just the start of the show. As people take their places, they give me side-glances, more curious than ever, but with a slight more awe than before. Even Todd, who is doing his best silent "I vant to zuck your blood" mime isn't attracting the normal attention. All eyes are on me. I stand behind the draping curtain, trying to quiet my mind until I hear my cue and walk out onto stage a man in love, a man with principles, a man who will suffer but doesn't know it yet, and a man who in the end will kill the bad guy and get the girl. Yeah, I'm feeling my Kung Fu power.

Chapter 19: Pity Kiss

The play does rock. When it is all done and we are lined up to take a bow, I look out to the faces, the clapping, the hooting, and bow again. The curtain closes.

Mrs. Halestrom gives us her version of a pep talk—get enough sleep, practice your lines, come tomorrow by 4:00 p.m., ready to "give the show of your lifetime." I think she practices delivering these lines in the mirror.

Trenton and Sarah walk in at the end of the speech and all attention is turned to them.

Mrs. Halestrom spaz claps and goes away as they walk toward me. I look when Michelle pushes up to me, grabbing my hand.

"Let's see this library," Trenton says but then notices my hand interlaced with Michelle's. I get the eyebrow lift.

"Trenton, Sarah, this is Michelle," I say.

Sarah smiles at Michelle. I can tell it is totally fake. "Hey," she says, stretching out her hand toward Michelle's.

Michelle lets go of my hand and shakes Sarah's. "Don't kiss my boyfriend again, okay?"

Trenton starts to laugh and catches himself. Sarah does laugh though. "Boyfriend?" she says and points at me. "Him?"

"Yes," Michelle says, very steady.

"Well, isn't this awkward," Trenton says. "Hey, red,

settle down. Sarah lip-locks with everything—even me, see?"

Trenton leans over and he and Sarah start to French and make obscene noises.

"That's lovely," Michelle says. She turns to me then, kisses my cheek and walks off. "I'll let you spend some time with your friends. See you tomorrow."

"Yep," I say.

It's kind of weird in the car. I forget they don't know shit about Eagle Peak.

"Okay, See," Trenton says. "I'm driving down this huge-ass hill. I assume that lame string of lights ending with the triangle impersonating a Christmas tree marks 'Main Street?'"

"Righto," I say.

"Jeezus! This is so much worse than I imagined," he says.

"Right."

"Shit," Sarah says—poignant as ever.

"Yep."

I direct Trenton to the library, and they silently follow me up the back stairs.

My parents aren't home yet, so Trenton and Sarah kind of poke around, help themselves to drinks and chips—finding Dad's stash of junk food.

We end up on the couch sitting with our legs pretzeled together as if we haven't been apart for like, forever. We talk about stupid stuff that matters. Trenton shares his most recent venture to a new club downtown that apparently epically failed in its attempt to create a toned down Gay '90s.

"First," he says, "the Gay '90s is, granted, dated, but

it's a classic! Second, shiny floors and painted walls don't make the drag queen singing "All the Single Ladies" classy—who wants classy anyway?"

Trenton saying this in his overalls, V-neck sweater combo is just too much and Sarah and I laugh.

Then I hear my parents coming up the stairs. They are shuffling, like they are really tired. When they walk in, they are smiling, but when they see Trenton and Sarah and I cuddled up on the couch, my mom beams. "Oh, just look at you three. My little cuddle bugs!" Then she throws herself across us, hugging us all at once. Trenton and Sarah are smiling and laughing a little as they get mauled by my mom. "It's so good to see you two!"

"You too, Mrs. A.," Trenton says, sounding a little strained under my mom's weight.

She gets up. "I'll make popcorn," she says and bounces to the kitchen.

"Wow," Sarah says. "She missed us then?"

The rest of the night is easy. I can tell they are bored and kind of itching to do something, but there really is nothing to do in this town, so we just take a walk around downtown and the neighborhoods. Trenton likes the metal triangular tree on Main Street and tries to climb but fails because it can't hold his weight. Sarah and I catch him and the tree before it falls.

We end up laying across my bed staring at the ceiling plotting a getaway for me to Minneapolis.

We are like this when my mom peeks in. "Luke's on the phone?" Like it's a question, which, I guess, it is.

I wave my arms dramatically. "Sure, why not?" She gives me a look which can only be interpreted as one of warning.

I get up and walk to the kitchen.

"Luke?" I say.

"Um, Sean. I need to talk to you," he says. He doesn't

sound altogether balanced right now.

"Okay." So talk!

"Can we, like, meet?" he asks.

"I guess, well, no, why don't you just come over. Trenton and Sarah, friends of mine, are here and I don't want to leave them."

"At your house? You want me to come there?"

"Yeah, I mean, if you want to talk." I am not going to make this easy for him. He comes to me.

There is a long pause. "Fine." And then he hangs up. It occurs to me that he might not know where I live, but then of course he does. Doesn't everyone?

I tell Trent and Sarah Luke is coming. Sarah shrugs and sits down in the living room in front of the TV. Trenton gets it though, and he gives me a pitying look before following Sarah. And Luke doesn't show up for an hour even though he lives like five blocks away. We are back in the bedroom when I hear the knock.

"You think this is a good idea?" I ask them weakly.

"Jesus, Sean, since when are you such a baby? Just be kind, okay?"

"Yeah," I say, angry that he thinks he has to tell me that.

Sarah and Trenton are walking out just as Luke is walking in. "Hey," Trenton says.

Luke looks a little startled at Trenton and doesn't say anything.

I sit back down on the bed. Luke stands in the middle of the room. He looks from my CDs to my Dead Kennedys poster to my clothes on the floor like he's trying to figure out what to talk about. I decide to put him out of his misery. "What do you want, Luke?"

He looks at me then like he's hungry, and I want to take back the question.

"Besides me?" I say smiling. I am trying to lighten

things up, but it's a bad joke. He looks at the door to make sure no one is listening in.

No one is, but he turns to leave anyway.

Shit! I can't leave it this way. I get up and begin to follow him.

He turns around quickly. "You don't know shit, Sean. How can you possibly know how this feels? Besides Lara and Todd, no one knows. Doesn't want to know. I kiss girls, and I even did it with them…"

Shit, this is deep. I feel like his life is kind of teetering, and I don't want to say the wrong thing—I realize I actually care.

"It feels… cheap," he continues. "And then you come, and, I mean, look at you, you have to be gay, and I think this could be it. Maybe I can just find out. But then you're not. And I'm like… Fuck!" He is pulling up on his short hair so it sticks up in random ways.

I sit on the bed and look at him.

He walks to me and sits on the bed, and I stiffen. He scares me.

"And you hate me," he says.

I look up. "I don't hate you."

"But you're scared of me," he says, and he reaches over to touch me.

To prove to him I'm not, I let him. His fingertips touch my wrist and slowly move up my arm, but when they get to my elbow I tense again and he pulls away.

"I'm not," I whisper. "I just… don't… want you like that."

Luke is looking down thoughtfully at his own hand. "I never touched anyone like that. It's so different with you. I can still feel you here." He brushes his thumb over his fingers that touched me.

I groan. "Luke, man, it's not me."

"What is it then?" he asks with so much anger that I move away.

"You're gay, Luke." I say. "Gay!"

He seems to deflate.

"Look," I sit up taller. "It can't be easy here. It's not easy for me either, but it doesn't seem to be easy for anyone, so stop feeling sorry for yourself."

He gets his air back and is glaring again.

"Luke," I say, grabbing his wrist. "You feel alone? Well, guess what? So does everyone. You think you won't be accepted? Well, if you keep hiding what you really are, you won't have anything. Not even you!" I realize after this diatribe that he isn't listening. Instead, he is staring down at my hand circling his wrist. Fuck! I let go.

"Sean?" he says quietly.

"Yeah?" Now he's going to thank me and go away. Now he's going to thank me and go away. It is my new chant.

"Can you do something for me? Just once."

He's not going to thank me and go away.

"Maybe," I say.

"Just once, can I kiss you?"

I pull away now and back as far away as the bed will allow. "Luke, I'm not even gay! Christ, can't you ask Trenton?"

"Him?" he says looking with horror to the door. "But he's like really really gay, and..."

"Black?" I fill in.

"Yeah, and I don't know him."

I sit up, hoping some height will help.

"Please, Sean. I may never get the chance to kiss someone I really like," and his voice cracks. I want to tell him of course he will. That he will have lots of boyfriends. I want to tell him about the Gay Nineties, about the gay coffee shops, about the gay pride parade, about the gay alliances at colleges, but I know he can't hear that now. What the hell. Maybe a peck will make him realize how unmagical straight lips can be!

"Okay, Luke. Once. But that is it. It won't go anywhere else." I can't believe the words that are coming out of my mouth.

Luke looks completely shocked. "Really?" he whispers and looks at the door again.

"Once, Luke. Make it quick," I say before I lose my nerve.

He slides toward me then. I close my eyes. I don't want to see his. I can feel his hand on my neck, under my ear kind of caressing lightly, and for a second I wonder if he's going to choke me. But then his lips are on mine and I squeeze my eyes shut tighter. Before he can, holy shit, stick his tongue in my mouth or something, I pull away and open my eyes. He is staring at me. His nose almost touching mine. There are tears forming in his eyes, but then he looks down, pushes off the bed and walks out of my room.

I hear my mom and dad say good-bye, but then the front door closes, so I assume he's gone. I breathe out, realizing I was holding my breath.

I sit like that for many minutes, just trying to breathe, breathe, breathe. I wonder if it was a mistake—if this is really what he needed.

When I finally walk out of my room, my parents are there, and so is Trenton. Sarah is already sleeping on the love seat. A kung fu movie is playing, but no one is joking. I know they want to know what happened, but they stay silent, staring at the TV. I walk by them to the bathroom and take a long shower.

Chapter 20: Play

There is no morning ritual on Saturday morning. Privacy isn't a concept that comes naturally to Trenton, so as soon as he is up, he is in my room, jumping on my bed. Perhaps bed bouncing is a fun way for some to wake up, but the circumstances are far from ideal. I wake in midflight and my back hits the bed nearly knocking the wind out of me. Add to that the swarm of memories about kissing Luke, and I can only swear and kind of groan.

"Oh, easy, boy," Trenton says as he hops off the bed and raises both arms. "What's wrong with you?"

Where to begin? I am too groggy to articulate a witty reply, so I get up and walk to the bathroom. Sarah is sitting staring blankly—does she always look like that in the morning?—kind of soft and warm, and Jesus, get a grip.

I can hear Mamma Mia playing as I walk back to my room, and I know that Trenton has found his old CD.

"I want it back," Trenton says as he cradles the pink case in his hands and dances. Now Sarah is jumping on my bed.

"Who gave you a caffeine shot?" I say to Sarah.

To Trenton I say, "I thought you have no need for the actual CDs anymore."

"I didn't, but there's something about having the case, you know?"

"Yeah, I know," I say, taking the high road.

And then we are dancing and it's nice. We close the door, crank up the volume, and dance like I can only do with Trenton. Sarah seems to fit right in with us—she always has, but I can tell her and Trenton have bonded over my absence—they even have some inside jokes as they dance, mimicking someone they must have seen while going out dancing together. I pretend I don't notice and just dance along.

We are making so much noise that we don't hear Michelle walk to the door, so when her mass of red hair appears in the doorway, we are all jolted and kind of freeze. She's not laughing at us even though we are frozen in very awkward positions. In fact, her eyes are all red and puffy, and I think, shit, what did I do?

"Hey, Red," Trenton says. I wince, hoping she doesn't get offended.

She doesn't. She seems to not hear it and walks slowly across the room to sit on my bed. I glare at Trenton, hopefully silencing him. Sarah is already walking out of my room.

I sit down beside Michelle and take her hand in mine.

She is just shaking her head back and forth, back and forth.

She starts mumbling something, but through the now sobs, all I hear is "...just died."

Trenton starts to back out of the room, but I look at him pleadingly to stay and he does.

"Who's dead?" I ask, listing every possibility in my head—Jasper, Luke, her dad, her brother? Luke? Luke? I keep coming back to Luke. I fucking killed Luke! I killed Luke.

Michelle is sobbing now, and I think about Luke's eyes as he pulled away from our kiss. Our kiss! Shit! He cried. I let him kiss me and he saw the glory of his gayness crushed in my nonresponse.

"Sam, well, Samantha," she says and starts whimpering again.

"Samantha?" I ask completely relieved it is no one that I know, but also sad that it is someone who Michelle clearly loves but that I don't know and it makes me realize how very little I know about her. But I can't shake the cold relief I feel and that makes me feel worse. I squeeze her hand.

"Sam..." she says with a sob that catches in the back of her throat. But she goes on. "Sam is, well, was, the calf I raised and won blue ribbons for at the state fair."

And then I do the worst possible thing I could do. I laugh. Not much—it's more of a short guffaw, but the second it's out I realize my tragic, tragic error. Michelle quickly pulls her hand out of mine and stands. Trenton turns away and walks out of the room, but I can see his shoulders shaking and it makes me want to giggle, so I smile a little instead and cover my mouth with my hand.

Michelle is really glaring at me now. It's like slow motion when she lifts her arm and wipes it slowly across her running nose.

"I'm sorry, Michelle, I was just relieved." And yet another bad thing to say.

"Relieved?" She kind of squeaks.

There is no going back now.

"Yes," I say. "I am sorry you are so sad, but I was thinking of all these people I know, and I'm just relieved it's not a person, you know?"

"How can you be such an ass?" She asks. I get that it is a rhetorical question, so I don't answer.

"I mean, I am fine with your honesty. That's all good, but why the fuck you think it's okay to laugh at my loss is just, just... cold!"

"But I wasn't," I start but then I realize that was just

dumb. I shut up, finally.

"You know what, Sean? This," and she waves her hands around dramatically. "This is over!"

Everyone is quiet after Michelle leaves. They know I know I fucked up, so there's no need to get into it.

The apartment starts feeling completely oppressive, and my mom is trying to get all of us to a Buddhist meeting at the Hopkins', which none of us are particularly in the mood for, so I take Trenton and Sarah on one of the only outings I can think of—a walk into the country. My head is spinning about Michelle. I feel bad, but not bad enough. I feel like I should feel more after an official break-up. Really, I feel kind of free.

"There are like no bars in this town," Trenton says again, holding up his phone in protest.

"Haven't we established that, like, again and again?" Sarah jumps off the sidewalk to walk beside us down on Main Street.

"This is Sean's life we are talking about here," Trenton says. Yeah, as if. "Imagine being him, and not being able to even call while you are out for a walk. What if something happens? What if some farmer like comes and abducts us and chains us in his barn to rape and torture us?"

"You wish," Sarah laughs.

"Rape is not a laughing matter, Sarah!"

And now I am laughing because the ridiculous never fails to occur with Trenton. I love him for it, so I hug him, right there at the end of Main Street in front of the wiry fake Christmas tree, where the town meets the junkyard.

We walk out of town along the old railroad tracks, and Trenton keeps whistling "Stand By Me" which was funny the first five minutes, but has become beyond painful. Sarah is just gritting her teeth.

It's like déjà vu when I see them coming down the path

toward us. "Fuck," I say. "I've been here before."

Trenton and Sarah watch as the two muscled masses get closer. "Are those, like, tricycles?" Trenton asks.

"Three-wheelers," I say, calling up useless Eagle Peak data. "Todd, the guy on the right, is cool because he has three-wheelers. His Dad is like the town CPA, makes lots of money, and is an alcoholic asshole, so he has rich toys and doesn't care that three-wheelers are no longer legal. Bigger than the law, you know. 'I can beat the shit out of my son, and no one's gonna touch me.'" I don't say anything about Luke—I don't know what to say.

"Well," says Trenton. "Aren't you a wealth of knowledge!"

They stop in front of us. Luke looks at me, which is disconcerting because I expected that he wouldn't ever look at me again. And he's not aggressive. Maybe kind of sad, but not angry.

Todd looks at Sarah in a way I don't like, but what the hell, she's hot, and the yoga pants and Uggs with the tight jacket show off the body. And anyway, I don't have any kind of claim on her. Claim? What is wrong with me?

"Want a ride?" he asks Sarah. She smiles, *the* smile. The killer one—the instant boner one.

"Hell, yeah!" She starts to walk toward him.

"Um, Sarah, is this wise?" Trenton asks. "Remember?" He whispers like they can't hear, "Psycho farmer... abduction?"

"I'm not a farmer," Todd says flatly in a way I have come to expect and appreciate.

"Well, then," Trenton continues. "Go off with the young man who kicked our friend's ass."

"He didn't..." I begin at the same time as Todd says, "I didn't..." and then we smile.

"He didn't kick my ass!"

"Could have, but didn't." Todd smiles, but really he

187

is paying more attention to Sarah. She is climbing on the back of the three-wheeler.

"Well, what the hell," Trenton says, and walks to Luke.

Luke looks terrified. I mean, terrified!

"I don't bite, honey." Trenton puts a hand on his waist and swings a leg around Luke. He leans into Luke's neck. "Unless you want me to."

I am mortified for Luke, so late to almost come out and then to have to deal with Trenton. Luke is looking down at Trenton's arms that are now wrapped around his waist.

"Come on, Luke. Give the boy a ride." Todd punches the gas and shoots by me toward town with Sarah squealing. I move as Luke shoots forward to join Todd and turn to hear the happy screaming as they plunge into the ditch.

And then I'm alone, and it's kind of lame. Like, I'd like a ride too! I walk back toward town alone assuming they'll find their way home and won't end up tied to a post in anyone's barn.

When I hit the junkyard, I remember the Buddhist meeting. I find myself at the Hopkins' door thinking I wouldn't totally mind a few minutes of chanting.

I walk in, ditch my shoes and tiptoe upstairs, happy when I hear they are already chanting Daimoku, the part I like best. No one makes a big deal when I sit down and join—no one even looks, so it's easy to focus. When Lara hands me some beads that aren't mine, I slip them on and continue to chant.

It's all good until we stop. I have a nice chanting buzz going on when Gerald reaches for his secret stash of study material and pulls out a sheet of paper. I can hardly contain a groan when he begins to read: "Esho Funi means oneness of life and its environment. This signifies that life and its environment are not two, but one, contained in a single life-moment."

"I think I get this," my mom says. She sounds different, kind of intense.

"Okay," Janine says encouraging her. It becomes too much—I just came to chant!

"Well," I say, getting up. "I better get back to Trenton and Sarah."

No one pays much attention as I leave, but Lara does smile and kind of nods when I catch her eyes.

At home, I don't feel like being alone, so I grab my government notes and sit at the coffee table. After a while, my mom comes in smiling. She grabs a book and curls up beside me on the couch. I should be studying for the civics test on Monday, but really I'm just wondering what's going on with Sarah and Trenton. Then I notice the romance novel my mom is reading. On the cover, some herculean man is embracing a woman with long wavy brown hair—one hand is in her hair pulling it back and the other hand is just below her breast. I imagine the words on the page are something like "he kissed her deeply."

Trenton and Sarah come barging in breathless and high-pitched.

"He is like the cutest thing EVER!" Trenton says.

"Todd's not bad either." Sarah smiles. "Nothing personal, Sean, but Todd is ripped, like multiple hard bumps on that flat stomach—it's hot!"

"Hmm," I say, trying to ignore them and read my government notes.

"And those three-wheeler things are like, uhm, really really fun!" Sarah is more excited than she normally allows herself to be.

"They're coming over tonight," Trenton says. "We are having a party!"

My mom perks up. "Party? Did I hear a party in my home tonight?"

"Yes, come on, Mrs. A. It will be marvelous. A real social boost for this little reject." He points at me as if it wasn't clear enough.

"That little reject is my flesh and blood, Trenton, and I love him so much." She gets up and walks to me arms outstretched.

I let her hug me as Trenton says, "Yes, we all do, but is that enough? I mean, don't you want him to be, like, the prom king or something?"

"Dairy King," I say, and Sarah and Trenton just stare at me blankly. "Seriously. It's Dairy King."

They crack up.

My mom nods solemnly. "And yes, it has always been a dream to have a dairy king son."

"Well, then, let's start planning this party!" Trenton yells.

My mom and Trenton are off to the kitchen to plan. Sarah and I go to my bedroom. She reads her novel for her Russian Literature class, and I reread the chapter we will be tested on. It's nice to lay with her on my bed, touching but not sexual. Well, a little I guess, since she's gorgeous and I have a penis, but nothing is expected.

Michelle is the first person I see when I walk backstage. She is completely surrounded—Jasper is in the crowd. So is Lara. I take a deep breath and walk right up to her.

I can tell by the lack of glaring from others in the circle that they don't know about our break-up, which helps give me courage to take Michelle's hand.

"Give me a minute?" I ask.

She hesitates, and Jasper steps forward (so maybe it's

not true that no one knows), but she comes with me.

I try to be thoughtful about Jasper as I walk with her to the bleachers where everyone can see we are not making out. He still cares a lot. I don't care what Michelle admits to me. She knows it too.

We sit down on bright yellow cement bleachers that now just look dark orange—everything is darkened in this dim light of the backstage setting that is created with those massive navy curtains.

"Yeah?" Michelle says. I deserve that.

"Okay, so I'm sorry," I say, but it comes out kind of bitchy. "I'm an ass, and I don't do the relationship thing very well. The people who, like, stick with me are kind of asses too."

Michelle snorts. "I noticed."

But that's just mean. I can say that about Sarah and Trent, but she shouldn't. "Well, they aren't asses, but we are just, you know, honest."

"Oh, and I'm not?" Michelle stands to leave.

"No, that's not what I mean. Jesus, Michelle, just fucking sit down. I'd like to just say something, okay?"

She sits and looks at me like I grew a second head, but with a look of curiosity, not fear.

"I am trying to say that I like you a lot. I kind of like everything about you—you are hot and funny and you've got this hair that makes me crazy..." I drift off feeling like I've just said way too much.

"Go on," Michelle says primly, smiling as she crosses her legs and puts her hands over her knees. She looks past me—perhaps this was her character before she became the psycho vampiress... but I digress.

"I'd like you to be my friend and to see where it goes from there. We never gave that a chance. We just jumped in and maybe we weren't ready. Well, I was ready, I mean, I still am, you are, like, really a turn on. That hair pull thing you do…" again, TMI. Why the hell can't I just stop myself.

But when I look at Michelle, she is looking at me. "We can be friends, Sean. We can."

She gets up and starts walking away. I smile and follow her back to the huddle of nervous energy also known as "jitters." I don't get that at all—jitters is what you get from coffee; it's not the cold sweat panic you get from facing an audience. But I know that once those lights come on, it all works out.

And when the lights come on for Dracula, it is a wonderful thing.

I think the standing ovation from the fifty or so audience members is a little overkill, but hey, who am I to turn down another bow?

Chapter 21: Truth or Truth

My mom and Trenton, being who they are, have invited the entire play cast and their parents to our home for a "post play party." I, being who I am, am wearing my favorite new gold hoop earrings, my Dead Kennedys t-shirt and black skinny jeans and standing in the corner of my transformed living room like a complete reject, smiling and watching everyone else.

Dad is serving "kiddie drinks" at the bar to us and beer to the adults. Todd is standing beside him—I'm sure they're talking about power tools or something. My mom is fluttering around the room. Her music is on—Cab Calloway, of course. Trenton and Sarah are in the corner, mock dancing. Lindsey, Lara, Jasper, and Dan are sitting around the coffee table. Lara is doing the hair tuck thing with her mole and it is strangely endearing now. I'm in the corner. The whole scene should be horribly awkward, but it's really not. Everyone seems to be having a good time. I'm just not so sure how I fit into all this or if I do.

Then Luke walks in, and I can tell he wants to turn right back around. Trenton notices too, and sashays over to him, grabs his hand and pulls him toward Sarah. Luke is still clearly wanting to escape, but this doesn't faze Trenton at all. He just rubs a hand up and down Luke's arm and turns to talk with Sarah—breaking the poor guy in.

Then Michelle and her dad and Lucinda walk in.

Michelle sees me and walks my way, flanked by her parents. "I hate to say it, Sean," she says, "but this does prove once again how cool your parents are."

"Cool? Okay, Michelle," I say, smiling, but only a little. Her parents and I shake hands again. It's weird, and I wonder if they know we aren't a thing anymore. But then she kisses my cheek and says, "Can we talk?"

"Yeah, sure," I say.

As we walk to my bedroom, Lara's parents walk in.

My mom screeches out a "Janine!" and goes running over to hug them both. They come in looking as at ease as ever, hugging and greeting my parents and waving at me. I wave back as Michelle pulls me into my room.

She kisses me. "Can we do this?" she asks.

"What?" I ask, genuinely confused.

"Be friends and kiss sometimes? And other stuff?"

I'm thinking, shit, this is like perfection, but then I get kind of a sick feeling that I can't even name. "You mean fuck buddies?" I say. I sound angry, but that's not exactly the feeling either.

"I said nothing about fucking. When and if I ever choose to make love with you or anyone else, it will be way beyond fuck buddy status."

I want to ask about blowjobs but stop myself. I immediately feel like an ass. I'm not sure what the hell she wants from me. She looks so damn cute, those big pixie eyes and the fiery hair in all directions.

"I don't understand." I say.

"God, Sean, just relax! This isn't a big deal. I'm just trying to make this all okay, you know?"

"Make it okay?" I still don't get this.

"Yeah, you know, let's just be friends, because clearly you aren't, like, wanting to be exclusive." She looks down.

"Michelle, I'm sorry." What else can I say?

"It's okay. Just forget it." She starts to walk out of the room.

She is almost too far when I grab her, so we trip into each other. I hug her really close. I bury my face in her curls and breathe in. And then we both let go and return to the party.

The adults finally leave, my parents going off to Eagle Peak Liquor with Janine and Gerald, so we are alone. Trenton and Michelle are dancing in the doorway to "I Will Survive," and Luke is just lingering near Trenton. I think he's unsure of what to do, but Trenton is kind and patient and pushy, and he keeps touching Luke's hand or shoulder and smiling. Luke has stopped cringing. No one seems particularly concerned about these exchanges, and that helps.

Lara is standing in the corner watching everyone. It seems we have that in common too. Dan, Lindsey, and Jasper are huddled by my closet. Todd is standing beside my bed, staring at and talking to Sarah, who is sprawled out on her back. I am standing here at my window, waiting. All the friends in my life. Funny, but I never thought this is what would happen in Eagle Peak. Perhaps it was the play. Perhaps it was Luke. Whatever. We're here, and we're together.

The song ends. "So, you all ready?" I ask.

Michelle perks up. "Oh, yeah, we are! And if you need a push on the ass to get back in, don't ask Sean. He'll just try to cop a feel—one push on each cheek and you'll go flying through his window," she says, smiling at me.

"Really?" Sarah asks. "On each cheek? That was sweet of him."

I roll my eyes at my smartass friend. I sense we are all

waiting for something to happen, so I open the window. The cold air whips in. I push myself up like I've done hundreds of times. I'm through the window in one fluid movement, and I wonder if everyone is impressed.

They're not.

"You expect us to do that?" Trenton squeaks.

"Yes," I yell from the other roof.

Not surprisingly, Michelle's mass of red curls is first out the window. She does it pretty well, and she grabs me when she is across, kissing me quickly before bouncing off toward the roof over the senior center, to my spot.

Next, Lara pokes her head out and scowls a little. "This is kind of dangerous," she says after looking down between the buildings.

"Kind of," I say. "I won't let you fall."

"Okay, just no hands on butt cheeks, okay?"

"I'll try to resist," I say smiling, glad that we can talk this way now.

Dan, Jasper, and Todd are next.

Sarah and Lindsey follow them. No one falls to his or her death, and before I know it, everyone is sitting in a tight circle in the tiny loft space that used to be mine alone.

We have the space heater going, but it's still cold. We huddle together in our little circle of freaks. It's quiet at first, kind of awkward, and then it's not. We laugh. I giggle. Trenton grabs my hand and kisses it. His other hand is rubbing Luke's thigh, and I am surprised that Luke is letting him. It seems a bold public move even for Trent.

The laughter dies down to chuckles. Todd is sitting between, yes, between, Sarah and Lara. Michelle is next to Lara, and her legs are wrapped toward me around my butt. Dan, Lindsey and even Jasper are huddled between Sarah and Luke. It's tight. Literally.

"Let's do it!" Lara says.

"Do what?" Todd asks. Then he smiles and slides his hand up her thigh. "It?"

"No." She pushes his hand away. "Let's play truth."

"Isn't it truth or truth?" Lindsey asks.

"Whatever, let's play." Lara points at Dan. "You first, truth or truth."

"Why me?" he says. Lindsey puts an arm around him. He continues to glare at Lara.

"Truth or truth, Dan. Come on. The sooner we play this damn game, the sooner we can go inside where it's warm and there's music!" Michelle yells.

"Okay, okay, I still sleep with a teddy bear." There is silence. I can't decide if I should be embarrassed for him or not. It's such a simple thing, but the way he said it all defensive is like, I don't know, really funny.

But no one laughs or responds. Those are the rules of the game. I see Jasper smiling down into his lap though.

"Truth or truth, Jasper," Dan says.

Jasper lets out a breath and a little laughter escapes with it. Then he looks right at Michelle. "Well, that's easy. I... love Michelle. I always have!" Silence. We all know this, but hats off to him for being able to look her in the eye given the circumstances. Her legs move fractionally away from me. I'm sure no one notices, but I can feel the cold air on my ass now. Jasper goes on. "Truth or truth, Michelle."

Michelle sits up straight, looking straight at Jasper. "I applied to the Perpich Arts School in the cities for next year, and they accepted me."

"What?" Jasper whispers. "You can't just drop that on me here."

Lara speaks up. "Hey, let's finish this. Michelle?"

"Okay," Michelle says softly. "Lara, truth or truth."

Lara smiles. "You all know this already, but I've never

actually said it publicly. I'm Buddhist."

Everyone stays quiet. "Truth or truth, Trenton."

"I'm gay," he says, and then starts to laugh. "Just kidding. I mean, I'm not. I am gay," he says this staring at Luke. Luke looks away. "But what I really want to say, what you might not know about me is..." A dramatic pause. "I've never been in love with Sean." A couple of chuckles erupt. Leave it to Trenton.

"Todd," he says. "Truth or truth."

Todd looks up at Trenton, right into his eyes, and says totally dead-pan. "My dad beats me, and I want to kill him." No one says a thing. "Sarah," Todd says looking down. "Truth or truth."

"Well, shit, I don't know. I mean, I don't know. Yeah, that's my truth. I don't know." Sarah looks at Lindsey and points at her. "Truth or truth."

Lindsey smiles, but then her face gets really serious. She takes a deep breath and says, "I've always wanted to be a lawyer, but I don't think I'm smart enough." There are tears in her eyes.

Dan kisses her cheek and whispers, "Of course you are."

I can tell she doesn't believe it though, even though he said it. She lets the tears fall down her cheek, and Lara reaches across the circle to squeeze her hand. "Truth or truth, Luke," Lindsey says, not looking up.

"I'm fucking gay," he says. His voice is strong, but it shakes. No one moves or says a thing. "Fuck!" he yells looking down at Trenton's hand still on his thigh. Then he puts his hand on Trenton's. "Um, Sean, truth or truth."

I look at Luke until he looks back. Then I look around the circle. Trenton is still beaming at Luke's PDA. Dan is holding a crying Lindsey. Jasper sits alone and quiet, glaring at Michelle. Sarah is staring at me. Lara looks from Lindsey to Luke and to me. She has tears in her eyes.

Todd is looking at Luke. Michelle is turned toward me now. They are waiting. For me! It feels a bit like preparing to deliver a line, but it's different than being Jonathan or any other character on stage. It's just me, so I try to say a truth.

"I don't mind Eagle Peak. Okay, no, that's not right. I like it, well, this. I like this. I like you... guys," I say, motioning to everyone. I can't think of how else to say it. It didn't come out right, but no one laughs, and I feel something so strong I want to turn away, but I don't.

Epilogue

They insisted. I told them they were crazy, that it was slippery, dangerous, COLD, but they said if I could do it, they could. When my dad showed up for our rooftop adventure to the little room above the Eagle Peak Senior Citizens Center with an extra-long extension cord and a space heater, I was torn between awe and annoyance.

So now we are here, my mom, my dad, and me. Our crazy clan. We are all huddled around the space heater, but it's still colder than shit. Wait, shit is warm. No, it's like freeze your eyelids shut and booger icicle cold. Boogercicle should be a word. Don't ask me how I know this is even possible.

"So, you are willing to leave all this?" my dad says, waving to the dirty walls and ceiling of my hangout.

"What," I say, "are we moving to Florida?"

"You know what I mean, Sean. If we move, you won't be able to come up here anymore."

I nod a little, but really, whether or not I can go through my window is irrelevant to my coming to this spot, my spot. There are so many other ways to get to these roofs, and I know them all. There have been so many nights of exploring. I even have a homemade rope ladder stashed over the Eagle Peak Bank for quick, alternative escapes. Lindsey and Dan and Michelle helped me make it. Turns out Michelle is a knot master—who knew? "I'll be okay," I say.

They're talking about buying a real house in Eagle Peak, settling in. They are asking my permission, and I'm not even sure they know that is what they're doing. It's cute, really.

I stretch my legs out and notice my pants are getting shorter, or maybe I'm growing. That'd be cool. Maybe I'll even get Todd muscles. Naw, not without significant steroid use and weightlifting, and it just isn't worth it. Besides, I'm friends now with Eagle Peak's biggest badasses, Luke and Todd, so I'm covered. Then I remember Trenton and Sarah are due for a visit. Their love affairs with Luke and Todd have worked out pretty well for me. It assures they will keep visiting me even when I'm an ass, which is often.

My mom is staring at me. It's the maternal love stare, saved for "I'm so proud of you" or "That's my boy" moments. Why don't mothers realize that's the most awkward look ever? "What?" I ask.

She reaches out and moves my bangs, which hang way beyond my hat, out of the way. She has this need to see my eyes, like I can't lie to her when I'm looking in her eyes. But I'm an actor, and even my eyes can lie. But there is no need to lie tonight. I'm good.

"Are you happy?" She asks.

This is a normal question for her, but I know this isn't the normal happy people usually talk about. This is the Buddhist happy, which means, as far as I can decipher, something like, "Are you moving through your Karma?" It's an impossible question to answer, actually, so I usually just say yes. "Yes, Mom."

She smiles. She trusts that I know whether or not I'm moving through my karma. I'm still going to meetings at the Hopkins' with her, so that should keep me moving. I guess.

We sit in silence. The wind is rattling the old wood

planks that are the walls to this room, but the heat from the space heater is just enough to keep the boogercicles from forming.

"Your dad and I are wondering if you'd like to come with us this time."

I look at my dad. He nods. "Do you want to help us choose our home, Sean? You've got another year and a half here at least, so we want the next place to be good for you."

"I don't know, guys," I say. I am about to say something about living above a library in downtown Eagle Peak, that I totally trust their judgment. But of course that would be sarcastic and insincere, and they are looking pretty worried. So all I say is, "Yeah, I'd like to help."

But then because I'm Sean, I add, "And you two tend to make pretty whacked decisions without me!"

CPSIA information can be obtained at www.ICGtesting.com
Printed in the USA
BVOW04s2025180514

353836BV00013B/140/P